Broken Parallels

Shel Schneider

DEDICATION

For Wendy and Kathy. Thank you for supporting me as I took this journey. Thanks to you, I am not the same person I was when I began. I'm a better person because of you. Thank you.

BROKEN PARALLELS

Chapter 1

Leaving Home

Madena stood still as people rushed around her in the busy airport. She didn't have much money, but she wanted out of the Midwest more than anything. New York City would be a good place to go. She could be anything she wanted to be in a place like that. If she flew, she would be there before sunset, or she could take the bus and save money.

"The bus would give you time to plan." The voice in her head was soft and feminine. "But I know you're in a hurry."

As she turned to look at the waiting bus, the driver waved and held up seven fingers before tapping his watch. Seven minutes until he left.

Then the world blinked.

Madena didn't know how else to describe what happened. In a fraction of a second, everything stopped, went black, and came back. It blinked.

But one thing was different, she was now standing face to face with a girl who looked exactly like her. Before she could say a word, her twin shuffled past her and walked into the airport. Shaking her head, Madena walked to the bus. "Do I buy a ticket here or is there somewhere I need to go?"

With a smile, the driver waved her inside. "You don't need a ticket for this bus."

Halfway up the steps into the bus, she stopped and turned around. "It's okay," the voice said. "No one will harm you on this bus. I promise." Invisible hands turned her around and gave her a gentle push.

"Thank you." She smiled at the driver as she read his name tag. "Bob."

"What's your name?" he asked.

"Ma-" She thrust out her hand. "Call me Emma."

He shook her hand. "Nice to meet you, Emma. I suggest you sit near the front. I don't think you'll like the man sitting at the back."

She looked back and watched two girls stand and change seats to get away from a scruffy looking man. When he looked her way, a shiver ran down her spine. "Thanks."

"Don't worry, Emma. I won't let him bother you."

She tossed her bag in an empty window seat and sat by the aisle where she could see the driver. "How long will it take to get there?"

"Not long." It wasn't the answer she was looking for, but she remained silent. "We have one stop to make before we continue to New York."

Emma nodded. "When will we get there?"

"Soon."

In less than an hour, she felt the bus hit a bump. Looking out the window, she saw water. They were traveling on a long bridge over bright blue water. As the bus slowed, she thought she saw palm trees.

"Impossible," she whispered.

"What's that, Emma? Did you say something?" Bob stopped the bus and opened the door.

She stood and gaped at him. "There is no way we could travel to a tropical place like this in an hour. Not on a bus. How did we get here?"

Bob winked. "Magic." He stood. "Now hurry. Get some lunch in the diner. I need to take care of the ... gentleman ... back there. I won't leave without you, unless you want to stay."

Emma waited for the girls she saw earlier to exit before she slung her bag over her shoulder and hopped out. As she followed the signs and walked towards the diner, she bumped into someone. They both said, "Excuse me." They looked at each other and smiled. Emma was looking at someone identical to herself. "Just like at the airport," they said together.

Without another word, they walked together to the diner.

At the sound of the bell above the door, a man greeted them. "Good afternoon, ladies. I'm Edward. Welcome to our island. You may sit wherever you like, but first, may I take your photo?" He pointed to a wall full of photographs. "I place a picture on the wall of each set of twins I meet."

They smiled and posed with their arms around each other's waist. He took two photos with his instant camera and handed one to them. "Thanks."

He pulled a pen from his pocket. "May I have your name for the wall?"

"Emma."

He wrote it at the bottom of the picture and turned to take it to the wall.

"I'm Dawn."

He spun back to face them. "Really? The two of you have different names? I've never met twins on the island that didn't share the same name."

Dawn and Emma glanced at each other before Dawn spoke. "We actually have the same name, but I want people to call me Dawn."

"I want to be called Emma, and please don't ask for our real name."

Emma and Dawn sat together and ate lunch in silence until a loud bang from outside shook the building. They rushed to the window along with everyone else in the diner. Outside, the bus was rocking, and the back wheels lifted from the ground and slammed down with a deafening crash. After a moment of stillness, the door opened, and Bob shoved the creepy scruffy man out onto the pavement.

And the world blinked again. When it returned, the creepy man was gone, and Bob was climbing into the bus.

Dawn and Emma stared at the bus and turned to look back at Edward standing behind them. He shrugged and gestured to everyone else. They were all in their seats, eating as if nothing happened. "I saw it, but the others won't even remember that man."

"Do you know how we got here?" Dawn asked.

Edward shook his head. "No, but I've seen people appear and disappear several times over the last twenty years. Always twins like you, but that man didn't have a twin. Did he?"

"No. He wasn't, and Dawn and I aren't twins."

As Emma and Dawn sat to finish eating, Edward laughed. "I think I knew that. I don't think any of them have actually been twins, but I don't know what else to call them."

Dawn looked up at him. "Bob mentioned magic."

"That would explain so much." He bowed slightly and smiled. "I will let you ladies finish your meal. Order dessert if you like. It's always 'on the house' for twins." He winked and walked away.

"What happens now?" Dawn asked.

Emma sighed. "I guess we take the bus to New York."

Dawn didn't meet her gaze. "I think I want to stay here. I like this place." She looked up. "You go. Become a big star.

Chapter 2

Dawn's Journey in Her Own Words

Once upon a time …

There once was a girl …

It's been a long road …

Yeah. None of those sound right to me either. I'll just start at the beginning.

I grew up in a small town near a large city, too small for me. At least that's what I thought back then. On my way to find myself, I stumbled upon this even smaller town on an island. I've been here ever since.

Except that's not quite true either. Only part of me has been here all these years.

It's this island. It finds people who have a choice to make. I've seen it happen time and again. People live each possibility, choose the path that's right for them, and go on with their lives.

But this town wasn't prepared for someone like me. The two versions of myself should have stayed here until we decided, but the choices were to stay or go.

Someone might think I'm still here because she decided staying was better, or maybe because she never returned at all.

Wrong on both counts.

Every so often, she travels through, stops at the diner for dinner, and leaves town again. Each time, she leaves another version of herself in town. There are fifteen of us now.

It wouldn't be a problem, except for the fact that she's famous. Not just a little famous. She's the world-famous superstar, simply known as Emma, touring the world to share her music. The fifteen of us look just like her, but no one in this crazy town thinks it's weird at all. Of course, we don't go all out on hair, makeup, and clothes. So, we really look more like each other and less like Emma.

None of us know what choice needs to be made or if it needs to be fifteen choices now.

* * *

Sometimes I feel like I'm missing something with numbers two through fifteen. That's how we refer to ourselves. I should have been number one, but I call myself Dawn. It seemed fitting for my new life. The others call themselves Emma Two, Emma Three, and so on.

I'm not always included in social events. Not that I want to be. After all, that's why I stayed when Emma left town. I've been comfortable by myself. I work my job and have hobbies, but I stay away from everyone as much as I can. I like the quiet.

When I noticed Two through Five eating together at the diner every day, I began to wonder why. This was before Seven appeared, and no one had seen Six in weeks.

They gave me polite greetings when I ventured into the diner and sat at the counter near their table. As I ate my lunch, I heard that Six had tried to leave town. She vanished as she crossed the bridge at the edge of town along with the car she was driving. They assumed she was dead.

What's even more surprising is that no one else in town remembers her being here, except Edward and me. Everyone thinks there are five of us that are sisters. That's how the magic of this place seems to work. Only those duplicated by the magic know about the secret and only while under the spell. For me, it has been several years. I won't say how many because it's not polite to ask a woman her age.

But I digress.

There did seem to be something happening with Two through Five. I made it a point to be in the diner when they were there. That's how I came to be there when Emma came in again and brought Seven with her.

Seven immediately sat with the others, but Emma sat next to me at the counter. I shook being so close to someone so famous. It made no sense. She was me, but I didn't know how to behave around her.

With a smile, she leaned close and put her arm around my shoulders. It felt so much like the comforting hug of my mother, who I lost before coming to this town. She told me I was invited to join the group, but I declined. With a kiss to my cheek, she said she understood.

As she stood to join the others, she slipped me a paper with a phone number and email address and told me to contact her later.

Talking on the phone with her was a terrifying prospect. I put it off for weeks as I tried to compose an email. What was I supposed to say? How do you talk to yourself?

* * *

I guess I procrastinated too long because Emma actually called me. How she got my number, I don't know.

I almost dropped my phone when I realized it was her calling. Why was I star struck with myself?

My fear disappeared once we talked for a while. She needed someone to confide in, someone who wouldn't judge, someone who would listen. We talked for hours, and she listened as much to me as I did to her. I connected with her in a way I wanted to connect with the others.

She explained that they had been created during difficult times in her life, but I had been created when she was still young and innocent. Seven should be better, but Two through Five were working on special projects for her. She had spread herself thin, and they were able to help.

That explained why they all started looking even more like her, they were expected to be her at times. They helped behind the scenes, but with all the video calls, they had to look as much like her as possible.

I wonder if the people in town even noticed.

* * *

From then on, each time my Emma came to town, we would spend hours talking alone while the others did their own thing. She always left with a hug and a kiss on my cheek.

We talked on the phone weekly, but it wasn't the same, even with video calls. I missed her immensely between visits.

Once she confided that she wished she could come see me more often, but she didn't want the town overrun with hundreds of her doppelgängers. If only we knew a way to stop them from appearing. The only way I think would work would cause all of us, except for the one on the chosen path, to disappear. I suspected that would be her.

Of course, Two through Fifteen could attempt to leave town and see what happens. Then when she returns … I'm not sure I want to think about those possibilities.

* * *

I don't know who or what controls the magic in this town, but after several years without a visit from Emma, something changed. One by one, Two through Fifteen began to fade away and disappear.

Two disappeared first. Then the others disappeared in the same order they appeared. It took several months, but I was the only one still on the island.

I didn't think much of it until I couldn't reach Emma on the phone. I worried that she was gone too, but her music still played on the radio. There were no stories on the news about her being missing or dead.

Then, one day in the diner, I felt arms wrap around me and felt a soft kiss on my cheek. I spun around and cried at seeing her again. We hugged and cried together before talking late into the night.

Now it's daily phone calls, and she visits several times a year. I don't leave for fear of disappearing, but she plans to come back here to stay once she's ready to retire. Who knows what will happen then? Perhaps the magic will let us both stay.

Chapter 3

Cassie Meets Donna

Donna began life with another name the same as Emma, Dawn, and Maddie. It was a fine stage name, but she needed to separate herself from that persona in her downtime. Not that she had much time to herself. She didn't have help the way Emma did, and she absolutely had no time to find love. "I tried to bring her to the island where the magic would help her." The feminine voice spoke into the night even though no people were there to hear her on this island. This island had the same magic, but it existed in another world. This world's magic was more subtle, sending signs to guide people to their decisions.

"I tried to let her be, but there was a glitch. How do I fix it? Number Six didn't cause it, but she's caught up in it." The voice sighed, causing the ground to tremble. "Why did she take the car and leave the island? I don't understand."

"I don't understand either, Dear," a male voice said. "I tried to give that pop star a push in the right direction, but that one from your world showed up."

"I didn't ask for your help."

"I know, Dear, but I can never help myself. I'm a romantic. I found someone for her," he said. "You'll see. I have a plan."

"That's what worries me."

* * *

The first time Cassie heard that voice she tingled all over. It was one song on the radio heard through static. The song wasn't even that great, not that she heard the words. It was all about the feel of the music and that voice. She didn't even know who it was. She missed the DJ's intro for the song.

Obsessed with that voice, she saved her money and bought every album she could find. Not every song touched her the way the first one had, but the songs that did seemed like they were talking directly to her. There seemed to be at least one on each album.

Months later, when she won concert tickets from a radio station, and she heard that voice on the phone speaking her name, she fainted. After a fumbling catch of the phone, her friend explained what happened and accepted the prize for her.

"I can't go," she said, her voice shaking. "I might die if I see her up close."

"Maybe she'll give you mouth to mouth."

"That's not funny!" She knew her friend said it as a joke, but that thought terrified her.

* * *

Cassie blushed and choked on her words when she told the security guy at the door that she won tickets and needed to pick them up. Her friend stepped up again to rescue her. "Can I get them for her? I think she might collapse if she has to talk to more people."

"I can have them brought here for you." He signaled to someone across the room who rushed to bring the tickets. After verifying her identity, they were escorted to the front row.

"No. No. No." Cassie grabbed her head, tangling her fingers in her hair. "I can't be this close," she whispered. "Please. We can trade spots with someone."

"You'll be fine once the music starts."

And she was until those beautiful eyes stared right into hers. It was only a moment at first, but that gaze kept coming back to hers. She never realized how expressive someone could be with just their eyes.

Her friend was right. The music did make a difference. Something magical happened when she heard those special songs, and this concert was full of them.

Near the end, the beautiful goddess of a singer reached down and took her hand. When she let go, Cassie felt soft fingers graze her cheek.

She was frozen in place and stayed that way after the concert ended. It took several tries for her friend to snap her out of it.

When she got home, there was a video playing on her television, but the power was clearly off. The video was a loop of the hand hold and cheek touch, but it also showed something she didn't remember. Those soft fingers traveled straight from her cheek to the bright red lips singing to her.

She fainted again.

* * *

Donna knew it was never a good idea to sneak out this time of night in a strange city, but she had to get away from her tour crew. They were pressing in on her, suffocating her. She needed to breathe before they moved on to the next city.

She walked under a clear sky with the moon lighting her path. In the small city, she could walk down the center of the street without worry. She'd been there three days. This city went to sleep after midnight.

It was nice, until a speeding car almost ran her down. If it hadn't been for the headlights, she'd be dead. As the car sped by, she stumbled to the side of the road.

Instantly, she was wet, drenched from a downpour of rain. A moment before, there wasn't a cloud in the sky with a nearly full moon shining down on her. She looked around, the car was gone, the buildings had changed, and it was freezing.

When a flash of lightning lit up the sky, she ran to the nearest building. It was an apartment building, and she didn't think anyone would be awake at this hour. At least she was under the eaves and out of the rain, but the wind whipped her hair across her face.

Pulling out her phone, she tried to make a call, but it died before connecting. She swore a string of profanities, not caring at all who heard her.

As she stood shivering against the cold stone wall, she heard a door open. She squinted against the sudden light from the apartment.

"Do you want to come inside?"

The woman looked familiar, even though she was only wearing pajamas and slippers, but she couldn't place her.

"I'm Cassie, and you really should come inside. No one else is around, except my creepy landlord, James, and you don't want to meet him." She shivered. "My neighbors all work third shift at the factory, and the cops rarely drive by here. You'll be out here a long time." She motioned for her to come inside. "Please, I won't be able to sleep knowing you're out here in this storm."

She recognized Cassie now and accepted the invitation to go inside, but it wasn't much warmer. At least it was dry. "Thank you." Her voice broke as she spoke. "My phone died."

"Sorry it's not warm in here. The furnace is broken, and maintenance hasn't fixed it yet. I can make you a cup of hot tea. It will help your throat and warm you up." She started heating some water, before turning back around. "Can I ask your name?"

Cassie had no idea who was in her apartment, no idea they had heard each other before, seen each other before, even touched. There was no recognition. She just wanted to help someone in need. Clearly, she needed help herself based on the past due bills cluttering the tabletop.

She didn't want to frighten Cassie by giving the name her fans used. She remembered the anxiety over a touch at a concert years ago.

"You don't have to tell me," Cassie said. "But we need to get you out of those wet clothes. I have warm clothes you can wear."

"You can call me Donna." She started pulling off her clothes. To her surprise, Cassie didn't shy away, but her face did turn red when she helped unhook her bra. "I'm sorry. I'm shaking so much."

Cassie waved her hand. "I didn't even notice. Come with me. You need warm clothes. You can take what you like. I'm going to make the tea."

"Thank you." Donna nodded and grabbed a t-shirt, a hoodie, and a pair of sweatpants.

From the other room, Cassie shouted, "If you think they'll fit, you can wear my underwear and a bra."

Donna smiled as she grabbed some panties but not a bra and thought, *if she recognizes me later, she's going to have a massive anxiety attack*. She looked around the small bedroom as she dressed. A photo in a frame by the bed caught her attention. It was a shot from that concert where she touched Cassie's cheek. Next to it was a photo of Donna holding her fingers to her lips. "How did she get these?" she whispered as she ran her fingers along the tops of the framed photos.

They drank hot tea in awkward silence before Cassie said, "We need to warm you up more."

"We?" Donna smiled, but she was still shaking. "What do you have in mind?" She laughed when Cassie almost dropped her cup.

Cassie swallowed hard and coughed. "We need to get under the blankets and share body heat."

Donna smirked. "Okay, but who's in front, and who's behind."

Cassie coughed again. "Face to face, as close as we can. It really helps."

Donna knew she was right. She was no stranger to living in these conditions. She paid her dues before she was discovered.

"Okay," Donna said, "but I hope you don't snore."

* * *

Donna let Cassie sleep as she changed into her own clothes. The sun coming through the windows warmed the apartment. After a brief search, she found her phone where Cassie had left it to charge. With a couple swipes, she dialed.

When someone answered, she blurted out, "I'm in Michigan." She paced as she listened. "I don't know how I got here." She stopped and sent a text as she looked at the mail on the table. "I'm close to the next show venue. Send someone to get me, and they should bring …" She paused. "Yes. That's perfect, and I don't need security." She paced again. "I'm sure. No one will recognize me with how I look today."

Donna watched out the window for her ride and opened the door with a finger over her lips. Her driver nodded and handed her a package. "VIP and five hundred. Are you sure?" he asked.

Donna nodded. "Wait outside. I will be out in a couple minutes."

"Sound check is soon," he said.

"I know." She waited until she was alone in the room before she sat and looked through the bills. Five hundred dollars would just barely cover the past due amounts. She neatly stacked the bills and placed a VIP ticket for the show and the five hundred dollars on top. Not wanting to leave the apartment unlocked, she woke Cassie. "I need to leave," she said. "Come lock the door."

As a groggy Cassie started to shut the door behind her, she said, "Thank you, and I left something for you on the table." She hurried out to the car before Cassie realized what happened.

* * *

As usual, prepping to go onstage was chaos. Donna had her hair done and her makeup. She was partially through the wardrobe check, when she announced she had to go to the bathroom. Sometimes it was the only peace she could get before the show.

But this time she just wanted a minute to find out if Cassie had arrived. If she wasn't there, she was going to send someone for her.

Then it happened again, she found herself in the middle of the street with a car coming straight for her. The same moment she realized what happened, she was knocked out of the way. She thought her security had saved her, but she found herself leaning against a barricade in Cassie's arms. Again, the car was gone.

Cassie pushed away from her as her face turned red. "You. You're -"

Donna held up a hand to stop her. "I know who I am, and you just saved my life." She left unsaid that it was the second time in twenty-four hours. She didn't think Cassie had made the connection yet. Something shiny caught her eye, and she bent to pick up the VIP pass. "I think you dropped this."

Before either of them could say more, security grabbed Donna. In turn she grabbed Cassie's hand and pulled her along with them. "She comes with us." Her tone left no doubt that she would not allow argument.

In the short, hurried walk to the dressing room, social media exploded with images of the rescue. Donna came to a dead stop at an image on the phone of a girl passing out bottles of water. She snatched the phone from her and turned it off. "No social media while working."

The image was seared into her mind. The driver of the car looked just like herself. Thankfully, it was being reported as a publicity stunt. Well, she had a plan to wipe that image out of people's minds by the end of the show.

To Donna's relief, Cassie didn't ask questions. She let people shuffle her around, do her makeup and hair, and dress her in new clothes. She must have thought all VIPs received this treatment.

Donna insisted on making sure Cassie was properly seated in the best seat with stage access before she allowed the show to start. Several times, her crew asked if she was okay. She insisted she was fine even though she was trembling. She was starting to understand Cassie's anxiety, and she hoped her plan didn't send Cassie over the edge.

Once the show began, she had no time to worry about anything other than putting on a great show. She did look down into Cassie's eyes as frequently as she could, but she refrained from touching her hand.

In the middle of the show, Donna surprised everyone by asking for a guitar. "I would like to share a new song with you tonight. 'How new?' you ask. If it was any newer, it wouldn't be written yet." The crowd laughed and cheered. "You laugh, but this song is less than a day old."

I saw you years ago.
A crystal rose among the thorns.
I had to know if you were real.
I didn't know how fragile you were.
My touch nearly broke you.
I left so you could heal.
Never knew you watched me too.

The years flew by.
I found you again.
How did we get here?

Lightning all around.
You rescued me.
From the rain. From the wind.
You rescued me.

Frozen, shaking, shivering.
You didn't shy away.
Wrapped in your arms.
Warmed my body. Warmed my heart.

Your kindness didn't go unnoticed.
I wanted to tell you everything,
I became the shy one.

Wrapped in your arms.
Warmed my body. Warmed my heart.

Broke my heart to leave you.
Would I ever see you again?
My busy life called me away from you.
But I wanted to stay.
I wanted to stay.

I want to be in your arms.
Warm my body. Warm my heart.
You are my salvation.
Let me stay.
Let me stay.

The crowd, silent through the entire song, erupted in cheers and applause.

She waited until the crowd was silent again and signaled to her security as the guitar was taken away. When she saw Cassie was ready to come on stage, she smiled.

"You probably already know about the incident before the show. Social media spreads like wildfire. While I don't know about the car or driver, I will tell you it wasn't something I planned." She walked to the center of the stage. "I will also tell you that twice in the last twenty-four hours, my life was in danger." The crowd gasped. "Yes. I could have died."

She held her hand out and waited for Cassie to walk up and take it. "Twice, this woman saved my life." She saw surprise light up Cassie's eyes, but she didn't stop. "First, she gave me shelter in last night's storm. I was stranded outside with no phone or protection from the wind and rain. She took me in and warmed my body and my heart." She felt Cassie try to pull away, but she held tight, knowing it was her anxiety. Donna was feeling it too. "Then before the show, she pulled me out of the path of the speeding car with no thought about her own safety."

She squeezed Cassie's hand and smiled at her, ignoring the cheering crowd. "I never had a chance to properly thank you." The crowd was forgotten now. She barely heard them. Completely focused on Cassie, she tucked the microphone into a special pocket of her costume and stepped closer to her. "Thank you for saving my life." When Cassie leaned in a little, Donna pulled her close with a hand behind her head and kissed her softly. It wasn't the type of kiss performers do for show. It was a soft kiss that built in intensity until they both felt it down to their toes. She almost forgot where she was until the roar of the crowd was too much to take.

She helped Cassie to the edge of the stage, kissed the back of her hand, and resumed the show.

Chapter 4

Emma's Story

Emma cursed and slammed the car door shut before walking to the mechanics's shop. She composed herself and went inside. "Excuse me. Can you help with my car? It won't start." The young man looked up and stared, but he didn't answer. "Please, I'm on a tight schedule. Can you see if you can fix it for me, please?"

He nodded and mumbled something unintelligible. She laughed. "I guess I'm the last person you expected to see, but I need my car." Smiling, she placed the keys in his palm.

He attached a ticket to her keys. "I will take good care of your car."

She barely heard him as she walked outside, but before she made it very far, she heard the door open.

"Six is alive!"

She turned and stared at him, waiting.

"I saw her driving her car. Then it disappeared. The car disappeared and her too. But she came back. I saw her. She didn't die. I know police saw me by her car, but I didn't do anything. She's alive somewhere on the other side of the bridge."

Emma considered this a moment before walking back to him. She folded her hands around his. "Thank you," she whispered.

Crossing the street to the diner, Seven joined her. This wasn't a surprise. They were drawn to her. That's why Six's disappearance was so troubling. "Why did she leave?" Emma whispered.

Inside the diner, she was reminded that not all of them were drawn to her. Dawn sat alone at the counter, close enough to hear the others, but not close enough to look like she was intruding.

Ever so quietly and softly, she took a seat next to her. Putting her arm around her shoulders, she leaned close. The poor girl was shaking. "Would you like to join us at the table? There's plenty of room for you."

Dawn shook her head. "No. I'm fine here." She didn't look up.

"You can join me anytime. You're family, Dawn." She pulled a business card from her pocket and slid it in front of her on the counter. "Please call me, or email if you prefer."

Dawn was shaking harder. With a squeeze to her shoulder and a kiss to her cheek, Emma stood. For a moment, she considered tucking a stray wisp of hair behind Dawn's ear but decided against it.

With a sigh she sat with the others who were all too much like herself.

* * *

Weeks passed, but Emma didn't hear from Dawn. She didn't worry, but she did track down her phone number. The mechanic knew it, and it didn't take much to coax it out of him when she called. All it took was her name, and a sultry voice. Men were such pushovers sometimes.

Late on a Friday night, she made the call.

"Hello?" Dawn's voice was shaking.

In her silky-smooth voice, she asked, "Are you alright?" She heard rustling and imagined Dawn had almost dropped her phone. Smiling, she waited for a response.

"I'm fine." After a much too long pause, she asked, "I took too long to call, didn't I?"

Emma laughed a little. "Yes, but I'm impatient too." After an awkward silence, she asked. "Do you want to try a video call? It might be easier."

"No. Yes. I don't know how."

After a few minutes of trying and failing to get it working, they finally saw each other face to face. Dawn gasped at seeing Emma without makeup and fancy clothes. It was like looking in the mirror.

"I just want to talk without distractions, Dawn. I need someone I can confide in. Will you keep my secrets?" The pleading in Emma's eyes as she spoke brought tears to Dawn's eyes.

"I won't tell a soul."

They gazed into each other's eyes for a long time.

"This is really weird," they both said at once. Then they laughed together.

"So, what are we to each other?" Dawn asked. "I know we were the same person, but that's not really true anymore. We've lived different lives."

"I like to think of us as sisters," Emma said.

"And Two through Seven?" Dawn fidgeted in her seat.

"That's why I want to talk. You need to know that they all appeared after I became a star. They have that influence. It's not all good. Too much ambition and impulsiveness in all of them. Seven is better. She appeared once my life here was more under control. No thanks to two through six for trying to help me. I tried to do too much. I used them to make things easier, but it was just messier. But you … You're different. You appeared the instant I arrived here the first time. You were created at a more innocent time in my life."

Dawn's face turned red. "I remember that first day here. I only saw you for a short time before you left again. That was when the buses still ran through town."

Emma laughed. "I remember that day." She sipped a glass of wine. "Go get a drink and make yourself comfortable. I want to talk about so much."

They talked late into the night, and both woke up with smiles.

* * *

Emma paced at the foot of her bed in her New York apartment. She had attempted to call Dawn several times. Something tingled at the back of her mind. "Something is wrong." She grabbed her keys and headed for the garage. Before she walked too far, her phone rang. She almost dropped the phone as she answered. "Dawn?"

The male voice she heard from her phone spoke in a rush. "No. It's Edward from the diner. You need to come here as quickly as possible. Dawn is very sick."

Emma quickened her pace. "I'm coming now." She hung up without saying goodbye.

When she reached the garage, she waved her driver away, but her bodyguard climbed into the passenger seat. Not wanting to waste time arguing, she let him ride along. After a few minutes of driving through the city, he asked, "Where are we going?"

"I have to see Dawn. This is the only way to get there."

"You know we're going in circles?"

Emma grunted and nodded. "I drive and think about the island. The magic does the rest."

"Magic? Are you okay?" He reached for her hand but stopped when the car rumbled over a bridge that should not have been there. "Where are we?"

"You wouldn't believe me if I told you." Emma let go of the steering wheel when she felt it moving on its own. "I never arrived after dark. I don't know where to go, but the car does."

Her bodyguard grunted as the car sped up. "You know you sound crazy right now?"

She nodded and smiled. "I know, but you will understand when we reach the diner."

After a short, bumpy ride, they saw the glowing sign for the diner. Edward paced in the parking lot. The young man with him ran to get them when the car stopped. "Emma! Come quick! Papa is sick with worry for Dawn. The voice told us you would help her. Hurry!" He grabbed her hand and pulled her to the building behind the diner.

"I know the way, Eddie." She was almost running to keep up with the young man. Behind them, she heard Edward trying to explain the island to her bodyguard. "How long has Dawn been sick?"

"A couple hours. The man came right before it got dark. He made her sick." He opened the door and ran up the stairs to the second floor.

Emma gasped and grabbed the door frame for support when she reached the room, but she ran to the bed when she saw Dawn lying there covered in sweat and no color in her face.

"The voice says you need to take her outside." Eddie joined her at Dawn's bedside. "I can help."

"I'm fine." Dawn licked her lips. "I need a drink of water. So thirsty. Then I want to sleep."

Eddie looked into Emma's eyes. "Don't you hear the voice. It wants us to take Dawn outside. We can't let her sleep. She needs the fresh air outside."

"I don't hear a voice, but I agree. It's too hot in here." She felt Dawn's forehead. "And she's burning up."

While Eddie found some slippers, Emma helped Dawn sit. Once her feet were protected, they helped her stand. "We're going to the diner, Dawn. The water is better there." Eddie ducked his head under Dawn's arm. "Lean on me."

"How old are you now, Eddie?" Emma asked.

"I turned twelve last week."

"You're strong for your age," Emma said.

"He's smart too," Dawn mumbled.

On the way down the stairs, Edward met them and offered to carry Dawn, but Eddie refused. "She needs to walk. That's what the voice says."

Dawn looked up at Edward. "Mother says I need to stay awake."

"Mother?" Edward asked.

Emma shrugged.

"Maybe she's hallucinating?" the bodyguard suggested.

"No." Eddie looked to Emma. "The voice feels like it cares for us, like a mother."

"Guys. I need to hurry and get outside. I'm gonna throw up." Dawn coughed and heaved.

Edward grabbed her from Emma and Eddie. In seconds, they were outside on the ground. He held her hair out of the way as she vomited several times.

Eddie stared at the strange glowing colors flowing through the grass. "Is it supposed to look like that?"

Emma shook her head. "Run and get some cold water for her to drink and a cool wet towel."

Eddie ran straight to the diner and returned moments later as Dawn sat back on her heels. She sipped the offered water and swished it around before spitting it out. Then she gulped down the rest of the water. "Thanks." She waited as Emma washed her face. "I'm better, but we need to talk. Do you remember the creepy guy on the bus?"

As Edward nodded, Emma asked, "What bus?" She took Dawn's hand and squeezed it. "What are you talking about, Dawn?"

"When we decided not to take the plane to New York, we rode the bus, and it brought us here." Dawn pulled a wet strand of hair out of her mouth. "There was a creepy man sitting at the back of the bus."

Emma stared blankly at her a moment before her eyes widened. "Oh. That guy. That was ten years ago, but I remember. What about him?"

"He was here." She paused and stared into space. "Today." She pointed to the diner entrance. "He came into the diner, bumped into me, and disappeared."

"Disappeared?" Emma felt Dawn's cheek. "You feel cooler now."

"The fever didn't make me see him. He caused the fever. When he bumped into me, his fingers touched my arm. That's when I felt hot and sick, and he vanished. Ask Eddie. He was there."

Eddie handed her another glass of water. "I saw him. He was tall with long hair. He smelled bad too. Papa asked him to leave. That's when he bumped into Dawn and disappeared. Poof."

Emma sighed. "I suppose that if a car can bring me here from New York in a few minutes, then I can believe in a vanishing man." She helped Dawn to her feet. "What about the voice? You and Eddie heard it."

"You've heard it too, Emma. At the airport and on the bus. It's the reason you came here, the reason I'm here. It's a soft, feminine voice that reminds me of Mother. I don't hear her often, but she told me you would come save me today."

Emma was silent as they walked to the diner. No one spoke to her until they sat at the counter. "Well?" Edward asked.

"She told me I would be safe on the bus. Then the driver, Bob, kicked the creepy man off the bus. Then he disappeared. I remember."

Chapter 5

Cassie's Sudden Fame

Cassie felt something on her face and tried to brush it away. It was a hand. She opened her eyes to see Donna staring down at her. Still in a fog, she heard her say she was leaving. With a hand Donna helped her to her feet and to the door.

Cassie was certain it was a dream because some part of her believed Donna was someone else. Someone she had dreamed about for years. It was impossible. She knew that, but the feeling wouldn't leave her.

As she watched Donna through the window, she saw a car speed down the road. Time slowed, and for a moment she saw into the car. The driver looked exactly like Donna. Not just a little like her. Exactly.

Then time resumed normal speed.

"I'm going crazy. There's absolutely no way that was real."

Shaking her head to clear the remnants of sleep, she walked to the kitchen and stopped when she saw the money on the table. With it was a thank you note written in the most beautiful handwriting she'd ever seen, but that wasn't all. Under the cash was a ticket for VIP admission to the show that night. She'd never been able to afford tickets on her own, always hoping to win them. The last time, they weren't even good seats.

As she picked it up, realization flooded through her. She'd seen her crush naked and slept face to face with her all night. Dropping the ticket on the table, she rushed to the bathroom, dropped to her knees, and threw up in the toilet.

"Oh my god! What have I done?" She threw up again. "I can't go. Can I?" Shaking and drenched with sweat, she stood and washed her mouth out at the sink. She had to force down bile again when she saw her clothes neatly folded on the counter with another thank you note. "Oh god! She wore my underwear."

* * *

All day Cassie worried and watched out the window, waiting for a sign. "I don't know what I expect," she said as she tried to eat something. "It's not like the universe is gonna tell me what to do."

But then it did.

The speeding car was back, and it was heading towards the show location.

"Follow it." The voice was quiet in her head, but it was clear. She had to go. Two times on the way, the car sped past her as she walked the three blocks to the show.

Once there, Cassie saw Donna standing in the road with her perfect makeup and hair. "What are you doing? Get out of the way!" She tried a few times, but she couldn't be heard over the crowd gathered for the show.

Feeling a push from behind, she stumbled forward and grabbed Donna. She pulled her to the side of the road a second before the car sped past them. The only thing that kept them on their feet was the barrier used to control traffic. Her face was inches from Donna's. She pushed away when she realized she was hugging her tight.

What happened next was a complete blur as security grabbed the two of them and rushed them to safety. She was kept within eyesight of Donna as people surrounded her. They styled her hair and applied fresh makeup. Cassie didn't have time to be embarrassed as they peeled off her clothes and dressed her in something she could never hope to afford herself.

Once, she mentioned Donna and received confused looks all around. That was obviously a name she only gave Cassie. She knew it wasn't her real first name, but maybe it was her middle name. Cassie thought she knew so much about her, but she questioned all that after seeing this side of her.

Then it was show time. Donna squeezed her hand and smiled. "Don't wander off."

Cassie let herself be shown to her special spot in the audience. She enjoyed the show, but she shook and held her stomach the whole time. She wanted to run away, but she refused to disappoint Donna. The new song in the middle of the show almost knocked her over. She felt hundreds of butterflies in her stomach as she listened to the speech after the song.

She had no choice in going up onstage. She felt the little push again and the whispered voice in her head telling her to go. The crowd disappeared once she was standing face to face with Donna. There was no one in the world except the two of them.

Cassie was certain Donna thanked her for saving her life, but she was lost in those eyes, eyes she remembered from years ago. With the help of another invisible push, she learned forward. She was rewarded with an embrace as Donna's lips met hers. Awkwardly, Cassie put her hands on Donna's hips, but she felt her hand being moved up to caress her back. The world spun as the kiss lasted longer than she ever thought possible. She didn't even remember being escorted back to her seat, but she remembered the kiss to the back of her hand.

At the end of the show, security rushed her backstage where she met up with Donna. In no time, they were safely in her car and driving away.

"Tell her." The whisper in her head was insistent.

Cassie could barely get the words out, but she said, "I need to tell you. That was my very first kiss."

Before Donna had a chance to respond, the car screeched to a halt, landing her in Donna's lap. "What happened?" They both asked.

"You won't believe it," the driver said. "There's a car stopped sideways in the middle of the road with someone standing on it."

They got out to see and squeezed each other's hands when they saw the doppelgänger standing on the roof of the car bathed in light from the full moon.

* * *

It was after midnight, and there were no other vehicles to be seen. Donna looked behind them. Her security team and their cars were not there. Looking back at the woman standing on the top of the car blocking the road, she yelled, "What's going on here? Who are you?"

The woman appeared to say something, but they couldn't hear her. She slid down the windshield and hopped to the ground, fixing her skirt that had ridden up. "People call me Six in my world, but I prefer the name Maddie."

"Your world?" Cassie and Donna asked together.

Maddie nodded. "It's hard to explain." She paused and fidgeted with her skirt again. "Sorry. Nervous habit." She pulled the hem of her t-shirt down to cover the waist of the skirt.

Donna thought the outfit Maddie was wearing seemed familiar. It was so much like something she wore on one of her tours.

"Have you heard the voice inside your head?" Maddie blurted out.

"No," Donna said.

At the same time, Cassie said, "Yes. I've heard it."

"Do you think it's God?" Maddie asked. She played with the hem of her shirt. "Because I'm tired of being moved around like this. All I did was leave town. I couldn't take being around two through five. Dawn is nice, but she doesn't talk to anyone. Emma tried to help, but I knew more would come. So, when the voice told me to leave, I left, but it felt like I was being pulled in two directions."

Cassie felt panic rising in her stomach, or it could be bile. The last twenty-four hours had been crazy. She had opened up to Donna, but it took everything she had in her. She didn't think she could do it again so soon. She nearly fell over at the thought, catching herself with a hand on her knee. Donna still held her other hand.

Invisible hands lifted her and pushed her forward ever so gently. She expected the voice again, but she didn't hear it. When she stood still, she received a stronger push.

Cassie let go of Donna's hand and walked over to Maddie. "I don't know if the voice is God or not. Every time I heard it, I found Donna." Maddie frowned, and Cassie gestured behind her. "Because of the voice, I saved her life." Cassie grabbed Maddie's hands and stared into her eyes. Her breath caught in her throat. They were Donna's eyes, exactly. "What do you mean about your world? Where are you from?"

"The voice told me that I have to go back to my own universe. I don't belong here," Maddie said. "He was insistent about it." She looked down at the ground and kicked a rock.

"He?" Cassie let go of her hands and lifted her chin, looking in her eyes again. "My voice is a woman."

From behind, Cassie heard Donna clear her throat. "Can we all get in one car and go to the hotel now?"

"No!" The male voice came from all around them. They stumbled as the ground shook. "Maddie goes back to her world. You two stay here."

"Take their hands. Both of them." The quiet voice was in Cassie's head again. "I will deal with the loud, obnoxious one." Once Cassie had each of them by their hands, the voice said, "Don't let go of each other until all of you are in the car. Drive away. Direction doesn't matter. I will get you where you need to go. Then I can fix this mess."

"Is that her?" Donna asked. Cassie nodded as she led the way to the car.

The driver needed no urging to start driving once they shut the door. In minutes, the scenery changed, and they approached a bridge. A small group of people stood at the opposite end of the bridge. As they got closer, they saw two people identical to Donna and Maddie.

"That's Emma and Dawn," Maddie said. "This is my home."

BROKEN PARALLELS

Chapter 6

John Meets Maddie

"I don't know how Maddie ended up in this world. Driving across the bridge should have taken her to her own world, but she disappeared once she was on the other side." The feminine voice was silent a moment. "Why did she disappear that way? Why did she come here?"

"She didn't disappear, Dear." The male voice was louder than the female voice as he spoke, shaking the ground. "She was pulled into my world when I moved my pop star."

"Pulled in? That could explain things, but if I didn't do it, and you didn't do it, who did?"

"The mechanic?"

"I don't see how. John doesn't have that kind of power." The ground rumbled a bit. "If you say so, Dear."

* * *

John had heard stories about the island. People told him to stay away. It was full of ghosts. Everyone said so. That made it the perfect place to hide. His family wouldn't look for him on the haunted island.

Leaving his car at a shopping center, he walked to the bridge. It was late, but the moon lit his way. As he stared down the length of the bridge, contemplating his choices, a car sped towards him. He jumped out of the way just in time as the car slid to a stop where he'd been standing a second before. He watched as the car and the girl inside it vanished. He rubbed his eyes and shook his head as the car reappeared. In the moonlight, he saw a blond woman in the driver's seat. She looked at him and pounded on the window. She said something, but he couldn't hear her. Then the car took off down the road away from the bridge.

"What the hell just happened?" John walked back to the edge of the bridge. His decision made, he stepped forward and hit an invisible wall. He tried several times at different spots, but he was unable to step onto the bridge.

He jumped when he heard a car horn before a man asked him, "Need a lift?"

John looked over at an older man leaning out the window of a beat-up old truck. "I was trying to get to the island."

"I'm Edward. I own the diner in town." He gestured at the bridge. "The only way in or out is in a vehicle. The magic won't let you in on foot. Hop in. I'll give you a ride."

John hesitated a moment but opened the door and got into the truck. "I'm John. I don't suppose I could find a job on this island that doesn't involve being an accountant."

As the old truck rumbled over the bridge, Edward asked, "Is that what you're running away from?" He smiled when

John nodded. "There's plenty of work here. I know the mechanic across from my diner is looking for help. If you're good with your hands, he'll teach you. He's a fair man."

"That sounds perfect."

* * *

John was right. The mechanic job at the auto repair shop was the perfect opportunity. Tony, the owner of the shop, trained him to repair cars at first, but eventually taught him to repair so much more all over the island. He became a handyman. Then he learned to run the business. It took several years, but when Tony retired, John was ready to take over.

During his time learning his trade, he also learned about the town's residents. He was especially intrigued by all the blond women who looked exactly alike. Dawn, who helped Edward run the diner, looked like them too. John always got shivers when he saw them all sitting together in the diner. Two through Seven didn't have proper names. He wondered if these were the ghosts from the stories people at home told.

Before he came to town, the one called Six, disappeared. No one knew what happened to her. Edward and Dawn remembered her, and they were surprised that John asked about her at all. He shrugged it off as another anomaly of the island.

One day, as John sat thinking about Six, he saw a woman walk into the shop. She asked for help, but he was distracted by her appearance. He knew who she was. She was Emma, the famous superstar. He had seen her on tv, and he thought she was much too beautiful and famous to be in this crazy town. Then he realized she looked a little like Six. She smiled and repeated her request for help. She was having trouble starting her car.

Later, John wouldn't remember what either of them said, but he would remember her laughter and the soft feel of her hand as she gave him her keys.

As she left, he ran out and blurted that Six was alive. She stopped and slowly turned back to him, never saying a word. He knew she was waiting for him to say more, and he told her that Six disappeared but came back, he was sure she was alive out there somewhere.

He nearly fainted at what happened next. She walked to him, grabbed both his hands in hers, and whispered a thank you.

* * *

One evening years later, John wandered to the edge of town by the bridge. He enjoyed the sunset, but it was interrupted by blinding headlights and a car speeding over the bridge. He squinted when it stopped. Six was in the driver's seat, and she hadn't aged a day since he saw her years before, driving the same car.

As he approached the car, he saw that her knuckles were white as she gripped the steering wheel. He carefully opened the car door, thanking whatever gods were watching down on them that it was unlocked. He wanted her out of there before the car disappeared again.

Opening the door was easy, but prying her fingers off the wheel was next to impossible. Nothing worked. He sat back on his heels and watched her. She continued to stare straight ahead.

"Six, Emma has been worried sick about you," he said, putting a hand gently on her arm.

Without looking at him, she whispered, "Maddie."

"What?" He leaned closer.

"My name." She turned her head to look him in the eye. "I like to be called Maddie."

She blinked once, released her grip on the steering wheel, and fell into his arms.

John unbuckled the seat belt and pulled Maddie from the car. He left it running. Who knew what might happen if he touched the key?

As he kicked the door shut, he noticed the car was wet. The pavement around them was perfectly dry all around. "Did you drive through rain?" he asked.

Maddie nodded and groaned. "Rain and storm. Dark. Then daytime and dry. Now here."

He helped her to sit on a large rock at the end of the bridge. "How long were you driving? That car doesn't hold that much gas."

She shrugged. "Few minutes. Maybe ten. I don't know. I wasn't in control. The voice made me go."

He took her head in his hands and looked for blood. When he didn't see any, he ran his fingers through her hair to see if he felt blood. She laughed quietly at him. "I didn't hit my head."

He stared into her eyes, but in the fading light he couldn't see if there was anything wrong there. "Maddie, I guess I should introduce myself. I'm John. I run the auto repair shop." He backed up and looked her over. She was wearing a white t-shirt and a long plaid skirt. "How do you feel?"

"I'm hungry. What time is it? Is the diner still open?" She stood and twirled around. "I'm fine. I'm just famished."

"Of course, the diner's open," he said. "It's open twenty-four hours."

Maddie stopped and grabbed his arm. Her skirt swirled around her legs. "Since when?"

He shrugged. "I guess it was a few years back when Dawn put in the stage and karaoke machine."

She fidgeted with her t-shirt. "Dawn owns the diner? When did that happen? How long have I been gone, John?"

They walked in silence after John told her she'd been gone several years. He let her lead the way, knowing there was nothing he could say to help.

As soon as they walked inside, she was pulled into a hug. "I never thought I'd see you again." She pushed away enough to see the face. She didn't immediately recognize the face. "You still look so young. Where have you been?"

"Emma," John said. "It's a long, weird story."

"Where are the others?" Maddie asked.

"Dawn is in the kitchen taking care of business matters." She led Maddie to a table, the same one they used to sit at years before.

"The others?" Maddie tapped her foot and played with the hem of her shirt. "Are they here?"

"They disappeared. They weren't needed anymore. Dawn owns the diner. I'm here for a few days before I go back." She reached across the table and brushed hair out of her eyes. "I'm happy you didn't disappear."

The instant the words left her mouth, Maddie vanished.

Emma stood and turned to John. "What's going on? I know you know something."

"I'll explain on the way. Get Dawn. We need to get to the car at the bridge."

By the time they reached the bridge the moon was bright enough to light the bridge. The car was gone.

"What now?" Dawn asked.

Emma stared down the length of the bridge. "We wait."

* * *

The car speeding down the bridge towards them wasn't at all what John expected to see. It wasn't Maddie's car. Far from it in fact. It looked like a short limousine. After it stopped a few feet from them, three women rushed out the back door. Before the door could close, the car vanished.

Before them stood Maddie in her t-shirt and plaid skirt. Her long hair was a tangled mess. Next to her was a woman with an identical face wearing a bright colored dress covered in things that sparkled in the moonlight. She looked older than Maddie but younger than Emma and Dawn. In front of them was a woman who looked completely uncomfortable in the fancy clothes she was wearing. She looked ready to trip over her own feet. Her hair was disheveled too, but from the way she held the hand of the woman behind her, he suspected it was for a different reason than Maddie's hair.

It was silent except for the sound of everyone breathing. No one rushed to break the peace for a long time as each of them looked around at all the others.

John was first to speak. He raised his hand and simply said, "John."

The others followed his lead.

"Dawn." She raised her hand and smiled.

"Emma." She spoke loud and clear, almost like a mother speaking to her children.

"Maddie." Her voice shook as she swished her skirt around her legs.

"Donna." Her voice was also loud and clear, like someone accustomed to speaking to crowds of people.

"Cassie." Her voice cracked as she spoke. "Sorry. I'm Cassie." Her voice was smooth that time. She smiled when Donna squeezed her hand.

They stood, staring silently at each other for several minutes, until Emma finally spoke. Her voice cracked on the first attempt, but she cleared her throat and tried again. "I was worried about you." She held out her hands towards Maddie. "Again." Maddie rushed into her arms. "I hope we're done with this. My heart can't take anymore."

Maddie nodded. "You're like a mother to me." She squeezed her arms around Emma. "I didn't really want to go, but it was crowded, and the voice told me to go."

Emma looked to the others for an explanation as she rubbed Maddie's back. "You heard a voice? Was it familiar? Did it sound like family?"

Donna looked Emma in the eyes. "She thought it was the voice of God. I don't know who it was, but I'm certain it wasn't God."

Emma squinted her eyes and took a long, slow breath. "Anyone else hear this voice?"

Cassie raised her hand.

"Baby, you don't need to do that," Donna whispered in her ear. "You're not in school." She kissed Cassie's cheek.

Her face turning red, Cassie spoke. "Donna, Maddie, and I heard the male voice, but the female voice shut him up." When no one laughed, she continued. "Ever since I

48

can remember, I've felt pulled towards Donna, but I didn't have the courage. Things just kept happening that didn't make sense. I won contest after contest to go to concerts and charity events. Half the time, I never went because of my anxiety." She took a shaky breath and squeezed Donna's hand. "But a few days ago, I heard the female voice. She's gentle and kind and pushed me to find and help Donna. I saved her life."

"Twice," Donna said.

As Cassie waited for a response, they felt the ground shake. Everyone stumbled. Then he was there. No one could see him, but they felt him.

"You didn't listen to me!" The voice boomed and trees nearby shook with the force. "You could have been together years ago! You-!"

"You were told to stay away from my world." The quiet intensity in the distinctly feminine voice was worse than yelling. "I won't warn you again."

With a bright flash and a clap of thunder, the ground stopped shaking.

The female voice spoke again, softly, but none of them had trouble understanding. "I don't approve of his meddling. It always ends poorly." A glowing line appeared at the end of the bridge. "Don't cross the line until I come back to you. I need to fix his mess out there."

Maddie pushed away from Emma and looked towards the sky. She was shaking. "Will I vanish again? I don't want to go." A soft glow enveloped her, and she stilled. Occasionally, she nodded as tears fell down her cheeks. When the glow disappeared, everyone knew the voice was gone.

They all rushed to surround her. "She said I can stay. She wanted me to feel love and happiness. That's why she brought John here. She's sorry for the confusion, but she's trying to make a better world. It might take a while."

John pushed to the front of the circle around her and scooped her up into his arms.

"Let's go," Emma said. "We can discuss this in town."

As they walked back to town, Cassie asked. "Is Emma in charge?"

Dawn smiled. "Well, technically, she is the oldest of all of us."

Chapter 7

Finding a World

Dawn held the door open for everyone as they entered the diner. The power flickered a few times as they sat at a large table in the corner.

A young man rushed to greet them, hurriedly wiping his hands clean on a towel that he slung over his shoulder when he was finished. "I'm so sorry, Dawn. I don't know what's causing that. I'm afraid to cook anything right now."

"It's alright, Eddie. Bring us what you can. I'll get drinks for everyone." Dawn stood and patted his shoulder.

"Are you sure, Dawn?"

"She's sure," Emma said.

"Yes, Ma'am." When Emma glared at him, he said. "Sorry. Emma."

After he shuffled away. Emma laughed. "He has good manners, but I hate being called 'Ma'am.' Makes me feel old. His father understood that."

Cassie shivered. "Did you feel that?"

Donna nodded. "What happened? It wasn't a breeze, but something cold touched me."

Everyone murmured their agreement.

"I feel something else, too," Maddie said. "It feels like when the female voice surrounds me."

With a loud clunk, Dawn dropped a tray on the table. Drinks sloshed over the tops of the glasses. Emma pushed the tray fully onto the table from where it was hanging over the edge too much. "Dawn? Are you okay?"

Dawn shook her head and pointed out the window. They all looked. Gasps, murmurs of disbelief, and some cursing filled the room. "What is happening out there?" Dawn asked.

Snow, hail, sunshine, clouds, darkness, and more sunshine all happened in a few minutes. It was hot, cold, humid, dry, frigid, boiling, and then comfortable.

They all gathered by the window as it continued rapidly changing weather conditions outside. Inside, they felt protected, but there was electricity in the air.

"Did that really happen?" Cassie asked. "Weather doesn't do that, does it?" She held up her arm to show the hair on it all standing up.

Donna rubbed her arms and hugged her from behind. "I don't know, but I suppose we're stuck here for a while."

"I know there's strange things happening out there, but I have other questions." Cassie said. "Can we sit and talk?"

Emma nodded. "Yes. We need to talk."

"Before you ask questions, I want to tell everyone what the voice told me tonight," Maddie said. When no one objected, she continued. "I don't know what she is, but she told me to call her Mother. She didn't explain much, but she's trying to keep universes from crashing. I don't understand it, but she said there are too many universes because every decision made creates a new one. This town is her way of controlling decisions that would cause huge ripples and too many universes. Only this town gets duplicated for the people living here."

Silence hung over the group for a long time. Cassie was the first to speak again. "Did she bring Emma here?"

"I think so," Emma and Maddie answered together.

"John too," Maddie said.

"So, there are three of you," Cassie said. "You had two decisions to make."

"Oh no," Emma said. "I came to town fifteen times and created duplicates of myself. Eventually, all but Maddie and Dawn disappeared. I didn't need the others anymore. To be honest, I don't know what decision any of them represented, except for Dawn."

"Mother was kind enough to let Dawn stay," Maddie said. "Me too."

John scooted his chair closer to Maddie and put his arm around her shoulders. "It doesn't make sense, but I'm happy to be here."

"What does this have to do with the loud, obnoxious male voice?" Donna asked. "I'm sure he pulled me from where I was twice to send me to Cassie. I never heard his voice, but I felt him."

Maddie sipped some water. "Mother says he's losing his mind and can't remember things, but he was trying to play matchmaker. I think he was confused and pulled me along at the same time as you, but I don't know why I was pulled through time that way."

John cleared his throat. "I'm not claiming to know about science, if this is science. Maybe it's magic." When Maddie jabbed him with her elbow, he got to the point. "I read a lot of science fiction, and I wonder if our two worlds move at a different speed."

"That would explain so much," Cassie said. "But it doesn't seem consistent with Maddie's appearances and disappearances in each world."

"Distance," Emma said. Everyone stared at her. "It could be dependent on the distance Maddie traveled each time. I'm certain the universes are moving around, sometimes close, sometimes not."

Everyone was silent as they continued to stare at her.

"I do have interests other than music and dancing," Emma said.

After another long awkward silence, Cassie asked the question she'd been dying to know. "I know John and Maddie are meant to be together. We all see that. Donna and I are together." She gestured at Emma and Dawn. "What's your story? You're obviously two versions of the same person. Are there people in your lives?"

Dawn and Emma glanced at each other. Dawn gave them a nervous laugh, and Emma hugged her shoulders. "It's weird," Emma said. "I tried to find partners, even married and divorced twice. Maddie can confirm this. She was created after my second divorce. Since then, my only companion has been Dawn. She had always been alone."

"I didn't even socialize with the others that disappeared," Dawn said. She rested her head on Emma's shoulder.

"It's really not what you think," Emma said when she saw the look on Cassie's face.

"For a while it felt like having our mother here," Dawn said.

Emma nodded. "But now it's like we are sisters who are also best friends."

"The female voice feels like someone's mother." Cassie looked at Maddie. "Do you think-?"

"That the voice is our mother?" Maddie finished her question. "Is that possible?" She closed her eyes and wiped away tears.

The diner went completely dark for a moment before being filled with a warm glow. Standing at the door was a group of familiar faces. Two women who looked like Cassie and Donna and two children waved with awkward smiles. "She is our mother," the one who looked like Donna said.

Everyone tried to talk at once, but when the glow brightened, and they felt the caress of love, they went silent.

"My children, I love you all so much. I have fixed the world out there. My husband, who I met after I died, had another world he manipulated. The results were catastrophic this time, and I brought Candra and Monna here to be with you. Others from their world wait in town. I brought as many as I could.

"I know you have questions, and I want to answer the ones you are afraid to ask. The missing versions of Emma didn't die. They were absorbed back into you. Some went to Emma, some to Maddie, some to Dawn. They each had different qualities, and now each of you is unique. Cherish that. Donna, Cassie, the two of you are unique as well, distinct from Monna and Candra." The light around the new group pulsed a moment. "You each took a different path to get here." The glow became harsher with a tinge of red. "I am going to revoke my husband's magical powers before he causes more harm. I reset the world out there to the moment Maddie appeared. You can return anytime. Cassie and Donna's world as well as Emma's world are also accessible via the bridge."

After the light faded, Emma stood and hugged the newcomers as Dawn shouted, "Eddie, we need breakfast and coffee."

Chapter 8

Candra Tells Her Tale

I've never been a girly girl. I don't wear dresses or fancy shoes. All I need is jeans and a t-shirt. Sometimes I wear something with lace or ruffles if it's a special occasion. So, when I was paired with a woman wearing sweatpants and a hoodie for a special project at work, I was happy. I wouldn't need to pretend to know about fashion.

None of us knew exactly what this special project was. All we were told is that a group was doing research for an upcoming project for a celebrity whose identity was not disclosed.

I don't know what research could be done here. It's a factory. We make clothes for musicians, mostly local rock bands, but we sometimes get contracts for bigger, more popular bands. It's never been for anyone really famous. Once they make it big, they forget about our small business.

We were told the celebrity might come in to oversee things, and she would be incognito. We weren't supposed to disclose if we saw her and figured out who she was, and I didn't think much of it at the beginning.

On Monday morning, I had completely forgotten about the people coming to research, until someone pulled one of my earbuds out of my ear.

"What are you listening to?" The voice sounded rough, gravelly.

I glanced sideways to see a woman with blond hair pulled into a ponytail, wearing a black hoodie and sweatpants. She had my earbud in her ear.

"If you don't know by that song, then you've been living in a cave your whole life." I didn't mean to be rude, but who takes a person's earbud like that? "Sorry. I'm used to working alone." I try to get a good look at her, but she won't meet my gaze. "You should consider wearing a mask. The dust in here will make you lose your voice if you're not used to it. That's why your voice sounds that way."

"Thanks," she said as she handed the earbud back to me.

I didn't take it from her. "You don't have your own earbuds?"

"No." She shook her head but still wouldn't look directly at me.

Of course, I get a shy one to observe me. I wave her hand away. "Keep it. We can listen together. It makes the day go faster, but I only listen to one singer and only her live performances. I hope you're okay with that."

She nodded.

I went back to organizing my work for the day before I thought of what we were told in the meeting. "Are you going to be asking questions or just observing?"

"I might have questions."

It was awkward at first, but we settled into a rhythm. She silently observed me and occasionally helped with simple tasks. I saw that her name tag said Monna but didn't have a last name. I didn't have to tell her my name. Everyone walking by said, "Good morning, Candra."

After lunch, which we ate in silence, she asked her first question. "I noticed you don't listen to all the performances in the concerts. May I ask why?"

This was not what I expected. I thought she would ask about my work, not about my music, but I indulged her question. "Some songs speak to me. I feel connected to them. I can't explain it, but they're special. I skip the others."

"Some of them are a bit risqué for work. Doesn't that bother you?"

I tried to catch her eye, but she bent her head. She was wearing a mask, so I couldn't see if she was smiling. I really wish I could tell if she was horrified or just teasing. "If you don't like those songs, Monna, I can skip them."

She coughed and cleared her throat. "I like them."

For a moment, her voice sounded like I should know it. Was she THE celebrity? I was told it would be a woman. Who is this celebrity? Why would she visit a factory in the middle of nowhere? I couldn't imagine this shy woman being a celebrity. She wasn't even wearing jewelry or makeup.

"Okay," I said. "But tell me if you don't like something, and I'm Cassandra. Some people insist on calling me Cassie, but I like my friends to call me Candra."

Monna nodded. "So, we're friends?"

I felt my face get hot as I nodded.

We continued working together for another two days with her mostly observing, but sometimes helping. We talked about me almost the entire time. She wanted to know everything. I confided in her about secret fantasies I have, fantasies about the singer we listened to every day. I don't know why I felt I could tell her, except that she was easy to talk to. She didn't judge me.

At the end of shift on Wednesday, Monna told me she would see me on Thursday. On Thursday morning, I waited for her to take an earbud so she could hear a couple new live performances I discovered. By lunch time, I still hadn't seen her.

I changed my playlist during lunch, picking the fastest and angriest of the songs. I threw in a few breakup songs too because that's exactly how this felt. I know it's crazy, but I felt like we had a whole relationship and breakup in the span of a few days. I know it was my overactive imagination, but it felt real, and I loved having someone who seemed to understand me.

Near the end of the day, I heard her walk up to me, but I didn't look up.

"I'm sorry."

I could tell she was wearing the mask because of how muffled her voice was. I didn't respond.

She pulled one of my earbuds from my ear. I knocked it out of her hand. "Don't."

"I'm sorry," she said again. "I had a work thing I couldn't avoid, but I'm here now."

I risked a glance her way, just enough to see that she was wearing her hair down and wearing business clothes. I didn't want to see her eyes. After trying to see them all week, I didn't want to see them now. I wanted to be angry. If I saw her eyes, I might forgive her.

"Candra?" Her voice was clear and almost familiar. I knew she had removed her mask. "Please look at me."

I slammed my hand down on the table with enough force that the earbud rolled off onto the floor. "No! Go away! I don't want you here."

Monna placed her hand on mine. She had a fresh manicure with beautiful red nails. "Please," she said.

I pulled my hand out from under hers and shoved her arm away. "You don't get it. I don't want to see you."

She was standing so close, and I tried to ignore it. I could feel her body heat next to me. I heard her tap her nails on the table. Then I felt a soft hand under my chin turn my face to meet hers. I couldn't breathe. I was staring into the eyes of my superstar crush. "No. No. No. No. No. This can't be happening." I backed up and collided with a filing cabinet. "No. I told you everything." I was so close to throwing up. I leaned forward over the trash can. I felt her soft hands on my back.

"I'm sorry. I wanted to tell you." Her voice was soft, and she was so close. I could feel her lips move against my ear as she leaned over me.

I stood and shoved my way past her. "You can't toy with people's emotions like that." I realized I was still listening to music in my ear. I pulled out the earbud and tossed it on the table. "Leave me alone. You have no idea what you're doing to me. Go away!"

She stepped in front of me. "Give me a chance to explain. Please."

"No. I understand just fine. It was part of your job. It was all research, but you don't care who you hurt." I turned and took a step away.

In one swift movement, I found myself pulled into her arms with her lips pressed against mine. Her kiss was soft and insistent. I'd never kissed a woman before, but I had dreamed of it so many times. For a moment, I found myself responding to her touch. I even touched her cheek and held the back of her head.

Then reality crashed in on us. The factory was silent, and everyone was watching us. No one here knew I liked women this way.

I shoved her away, grabbed my phone and keys, and ran out the door.

* * *

I knew someone would follow me, but I made it inside my apartment and locked the door before anyone showed up. Sliding down the door to sit on the floor, I cried. "What do I do now? I can never go back."

I looked at my phone as it buzzed and rang. I couldn't even count the number of messages and missed calls. Then I heard a soft knock on my door.

"Candra?" It was my supervisor's voice, but I didn't answer him. "It's okay. You're not in trouble. I brought your things that you left at work."

"Leave them in the hall and go away." I knocked my hand against the door above my head. "I don't want to see anyone. I made a fool of myself."

"Not at all." His voice sounded like he had knelt down on the other side of the door. "We're worried about you!"

"Worried about me? I doubt it." I wiped tears from my eyes. "Everyone is going to hate me now."

"Why would you think that? You know more than half your coworkers are gay."

I wiped my nose on my sleeve. "I know, but this is different."

"Because of me?" It was Monna's voice.

"Yes!"

"Candra, it was one kiss. Everyone knows I kiss people all the time. It's innocent. People don't think anything negative about it."

"I'm going to leave you two alone," my supervisor said before I heard the telltale creak of the floor outside the apartment. I knew he'd walked away.

"That kiss today wasn't innocent," I said.

"Of course, it was," Monna said. "I kissed you to calm you down and distract you. I didn't touch you anywhere else, even though I know you have fantasies about that. I never knew you weren't out to your coworkers and friends. I never would have kissed you if I had known. With the way you talked to me and talked with others, I thought people knew."

"I've been afraid to tell people."

"May I come in?" Monna asked.

"No. I want to be alone."

"You shouldn't be alone right now. Please let me in."

I turned and ran my hand over the door, wondering exactly where she was in the hallway. "Are you afraid I'm going to hurt myself?"

I heard what sounded like fingernails tapping on the door. "Yes, and I will stay here until you let me in."

"You really think I will hurt myself?"

63

"It was a traumatic experience I caused. It hasn't fully hit you yet. I don't know what you might do. Please let me in."

I leaned forward and hugged my knees. "I don't want you here. I don't want anyone here. I want to be alone."

I heard the floor creak on the other side of the door, and I heard muffled voices and keys jangling. My heart pounded, but then I realized it was my neighbor opening his door.

Monna's voice was quiet on the other side of the door. "Your neighbor is concerned."

"He was probably just startled to see you outside my door." I wiped my nose on my sleeve again. "Go away. I'm fine."

"I know what 'fine' means. It's not good. I will stay here as long as necessary to be sure you're okay. I don't want to call for help, but if I think you need it, I will. I know you will hate me if I do that, but I want to make sure you see tomorrow. Please let me in."

Without a word, I reached up and unlocked the door before trying to stand, but my legs were shaking so much. I crawled away from the door as Monna opened it and came inside my apartment. I heard the click of the door being locked before I felt arms wrap around me.

"I'm so sorry, Candra. I never wanted to hurt you. I thought I was helping. I got to know you this week. You have a beautiful soul. I want to be here when that dark place comes for you."

I struggled to get to my feet, accepting her help.

"You didn't take anything, did you? Pills? Drugs?"

I shook my head. "No."

"Drink anything? Alcohol? Other bad things?"

"No." I let her lead me to my bedroom where she removed my shoes. "You really do think I might hurt myself, don't you?"

"I've seen it happen when people are outed before they're ready for it." I watched a tear roll down her cheek. "I am so sorry I did that to you. If I could take it back, I would."

"I'm sorry for yelling at you and leaving." I pulled off my socks with shaking hands. "I never expected to have you show up where I work, and then you kissed me."

Monna held up a pair of sweatpants. "Put these on. You won't be comfortable in those jeans."

I tried to unbutton my jeans, but my hands wouldn't stop shaking. "Help me."

Monna knelt in front of me and took my hands in hers. Her beautiful blue eyes stared into mine as she raised my hands to her lips and kissed them. "You're going to be okay. I won't let anything happen to you. I won't let the darkness take you. Not without a fight."

I watched as she unbuttoned my jeans and helped me slide them off. I should have been embarrassed, but there was nothing sexual about it. With a hand on her shoulder, I balanced myself as I stepped into the sweatpants she held for me. "Thanks." Sitting back on the bed, I watched as she changed into a pair of my sweatpants and t-shirt.

"Do you mind?" She asked as she changed.

"No." Watching her put on the shirt and slipping her bra off through the sleeves felt unreal. "Are you really here with me?" She knelt down in front of me again. "Is any of this real?"

"Candra." She held my face in both her hands and gazed into my eyes. "It's real. You're here. I'm here with you." She kissed my forehead before resting her hands on my shoulders. "I won't leave you alone." With a smile, she hooked a finger under my exposed bra strap. "Want help with this?"

"Please." I felt my face flush as she reached around and unhooked my bra before pulling the strap down my arm. Once free of one arm, she pulled it out through my other sleeve. I'm sure my face was red, but she didn't seem to notice.

After a few awkward moments I managed to lie down with her facing me. She pulled me into her arms, and I laid my head close to hers on the pillow. I could feel her breath on my face. "I can't go back to work. I can't show my face there." I choked back a sob as my tears started again. "What will they think of me?"

"They will think you are a beautiful person who fell in love." Monna hugged me tighter.

"Love?"

"That's what this is, isn't it, Candia?" Monna paused, taking a slow, even breath. "I know you loved me before I met you. It wasn't a fan infatuated with a celebrity. You saw my soul in my music. I saw myself through your eyes and ears this week. I've never felt love like that before."

"Monna, why did you really kiss me?"

"You needed it, but I'm sorry I did it in public that way. Do you forgive me?"

"Yes."

For several minutes, I let Monna hold me in silence. I felt her caress my arm and felt myself relaxing. Then I realized our legs were a tangled mess. I tried moving my legs, but being face to face made it difficult to find a position where my leg wasn't between hers or hers between mine. "My family would not approve."

"We're not doing anything wrong, Candra." She ran her hand through my hair and kissed my forehead. "This isn't sex. It's comfort."

I felt the tears start again. "You don't understand. I'm already a disappointment to my family. When they learn about this, I won't be able to face them." I hugged her tighter and squeezed my eyes shut. "They can never know."

"Are they that terrible?" She lifted my chin. "Open your eyes." When I opened them, I saw tears in her eyes. "What did they do to you?"

I shifted position to better see her face. As I did, I felt my breasts rub against hers and gasped. "I'm sorry." It was an automatic response. Anytime I ever accidentally touched a woman those words spill from my lips. I wasn't supposed to touch women.

"Candra, it's okay. Tell me what happened. Why are you afraid? How did they hurt you?"

"I was thirteen when I realized I loved my best friend, Liz. My family saw us holding hands. Holding hands. Nothing else. I was told it was inappropriate. Girls don't touch girls. No holding hands. No hugging. They said if I ever kissed a girl, they would send me off to camp to fix me. They gave me a chance to fix myself. It broke Liz's heart when I told her I couldn't even be her friend anymore. I didn't trust myself around her. I didn't want to get sent away. In high school, my brother and sister tried to fix me up with guys. They were always trying to feel me up. I couldn't refuse because they threatened to tell our parents that I still liked girls. So, I dated guys and tolerated their groping until I was able to move out and live by myself. By then, I didn't know how to act around women. If I bumped someone, I had to apologize instantly. I couldn't take the chance someone might think I did it on purpose."

Monna wiped away tears from both their eyes. "Then I showed up and kissed you. I am so sorry."

I told her all about Liz. She told me that secretly many of her songs were about women, but the lyrics were changed to be about men to make them more popular. She hated doing it, but those songs were written early in her career when she couldn't afford to take that chance. In some concerts she changed the words to the original which angered her manager.

We talked late into the night, and she gave me one more soft kiss as I finally drifted off to sleep.

* * *

Monna encouraged me to go to work on Friday. I didn't want to go, but knowing she would be there too made it easier. It was less traumatic than I imagined. I suppose my mind always goes to the worst case. My coworkers actually came around and wished me well, asking if I was okay or needed anything. Everyone hugged me. It was exhausting.

Monna was in meetings all morning to finalize whatever the secret project was. She never told me, and I didn't feel right asking.

After lunch, someone ran to my desk and grabbed my arm. I didn't recognize them, but when they mentioned Monna, I listened. "Monna is outside having a huge fight with her manager. He's angry that she turned off her phone and didn't take his calls. It sounds really bad."

I almost tripped as I ran outside, but I stopped when I saw Monna standing almost nose to nose with a man I didn't know.

"Some things are more important than tours, shows, rehearsals, or money. I couldn't be interrupted last night." Her voice was quiet but intense.

"You agreed to always take my calls." He screamed.

"It was unusual circumstances, Harvey." Monna's voice remained calm, but she spoke with more volume. She had to be heard over the murmur of the gathered crowd.

He looked over at me, and my skin crawled at the look in his eyes. "Is this your new bitch? Did you take her to bed last night?"

It happened so quickly that I almost missed it. Monna stepped back and punched him in the face so hard that he fell over. "You're fired!"

I ran to her faster than I thought possible, grabbed her in my arms, and kissed her in front of everyone.

I guess it is love after all.

Chapter 9

Monna and Candra's Flirtation with Magic

Candra was not prepared for how her life was about to change. Being outed at work, then realizing her work family loved and supported her, was a small change compared to the consequences of dating a celebrity.

Candra rarely saw the security team, but she knew they were always there. They never entered her apartment, but Monna said they took shifts outside. It was their job to protect Monna and, by extension, Candra. Uncomfortable as it was, Candra was thankful for it, but they had to learn to stay out of her way at her job.

Her job. That was more interesting in ways she didn't expect. It was a small business where they made custom order clothing, usually for individuals, but occasionally for groups. Most of the sewing was for musicians trying to make a unique look for themselves. Up and coming singers and bands wanted to stand out from the crowd. Candra guessed it wasn't a complete surprise that Monna had come to the company, but a small business would not be able to meet her needs. Later Candra learned that a charity had been set up to fund purchases for individuals or bands who showed promise but didn't have the budget for what they needed. It made Candra love her even more.

While Candra was part of a team that created unique clothing, she did not work in a sweatshop. She would be the first to tell you that. Everyone knew everyone there, and it was common to greet coworkers with a hug and sometimes a kiss on the cheek. So, when Monna came in several times a week to see her and observe the work, she became part of the family. No one thought it was strange to hug her or exchange a kiss on the cheek with her.

After several weeks of this routine and going out to dinner or night clubs a few times a week, Candra wondered where it was heading. Eating lunch together in the break room, Candra gathered her courage to ask. "Monna, what's going to happen with us?" When all she got was a puzzled expression, she continued her questions. "When will you be leaving? Going back to your home? You can't want to stay here in the midwest forever. Is this just a fling for you?"

Monna scooted her chair closer to Candra and put her arm around her waist. "A fling? Absolutely not. I'm trying to decide what to do. I know you love working here. It's obvious that you love your job and your friends. I don't want to take you away."

Candra turned to look into Monna's eyes. "But …?

"But I have a job in New York. I have a tour starting this summer. I need to start rehearsals soon. I need to hire a new manager. I wish there was a way to clone myself. There's so much to do, but I also want to stay here with you." She sighed. "I actually thought of giving it all up. The fame. The fans."

"The music?" Candra asked.

"Never the music. I would still make music, but it would only be for you." She kissed Candra's cheek.

"How would you make money? What you have won't last forever." Candra tucked a strand of hair behind Monna's ear.

"I've invested in this company." She waved her hand around. "I believe they will continue to grow."

Candra nodded. After a moment of silence, she said, "I tried to contact my sister again. I think you're right. I need to face my family sooner rather than later. She won't respond to my texts or calls. I think she saw that video someone posted of us kissing. I know she doesn't approve, but I hate that she won't talk to me at all now."

"What about your brother?" Monna asked.

"I don't have his number, and he's ignoring me on social media." She leaned into Monna's embrace. "I want them to be happy for me."

Candra's phone vibrated on the table. After a quick glance, she grabbed her phone and stood. "We need to go to the hospital. My brother-in-law was in an accident, and my sister wants me there." Her hands were shaking so much, she dropped the phone. Monna caught it before it hit the floor.

"You are not driving. My security team will take us." Monna stood and wrapped her arm around Candra's waist. "Don't worry about your things here. I'll get someone to bring them to us. Okay?"

Candra let Monna lead her outside.

After a mostly silent ride to the hospital, Candra had trouble getting out of the car. She was shaking all over, but Monna helped. People all around stared at them, but the security team kept everyone at a safe distance. The sound of people talking grew louder the farther they traveled into the hospital. Candra knew people would be taking videos of them. It wasn't every day that a world-famous celebrity walked into the emergency room in a small town like this one.

When Candra saw her brother and sister, she stopped in her tracks. "I can't do this. Look at how they're staring at us." She turned, but Monna spun her back around and gave a push.

"I will wait here."

Candra slowly walked to her family with security on each side. She almost cried when her sister pulled her into a hug. "What happened?"

"He had a heart attack while driving. They're running tests now, but they think he'll need surgery," her sister said.

"Car's a complete loss," her brother said. "He's lucky to be alive."

Candra gently pulled away from her sister. "I was surprised you contacted me. I didn't think you guys would want to see me."

Her brother looked over at the crowd gathering around Monna. "Is that really her? Or-?"

"Or what?" Candra asked. "Do you think she's an impersonator? Look at the security."

"Yeah," her sister said. "I was wondering about these men."

Candra took a step back. "Well, I'm dating her. I need security now."

Her brother laughed. "Dating? You're delusional."

"It's just a phase, you'll get over it," her sister said.

Candra huffed. "I may be younger than both of you, but I'm forty-five, a grown woman. I know what I want. This is not a phase." She turned to leave, but her brother grabbed her arm.

One of the security men grabbed him. "Let go! Now! Or you will be charged with assault."

"She's my sister."

"Now."

Candra felt him release her arm, and she walked back to Monna without looking back.

Monna took her face in both hands and kissed her softly. "Stay here. I want to talk to them. What are their names?"

"It doesn't matter. They're not my family anymore."

Monna nodded, kissed her again, and walked over to where security was holding back Candra's brother and sister. "Do you have any idea what this woman has been through in the last few weeks? She was terrified to see you, but when she saw your message, she came to see you because you're family. She thought that meant something. Obviously, you still treat her like a child. You can't accept the fact that she loves a woman. It's not something she can turn off. It's not a phase. I've had many long conversations with her. She's been attracted to women since she was thirteen. She never told anyone because she was afraid, and now I see why. I'm sorry about your husband, but I'll be taking Candra home now. She doesn't need your judgment."

With her head held high, Monna turned and walked away from them, straight back to Candra. "Everyone has their phones out." Candra whispered. "It will be all over social media."

"Are you okay?" Monna asked.

Candra nodded, wrapped her arms around Monna's neck and kissed her. The crowd around them cheered, and Candra felt her face flush.

* * *

In the car, Monna asked, "Does your family know where you live and work?"

Candra wrinkled her brow. "Yes. You don't think they'll try to come after us, do you?"

Monna hugged her. "I don't want to find out." She leaned forward to speak with the driver. "Take us to the hotel." She leaned back and kissed Candra on the cheek. "It's about time you met my children anyway. They've been asking about you."

"Your children?" Candra asked. "Lara and Ricky?"

"Yes. Lara is an adult now, but she still travels with me sometimes. Ricky is a teenager. He's a handful. Lara helps keep him in line." She squeezed Candra's hand. "Don't worry. They'll love you."

Monna was right. Lara and Ricky greeted Candra with smiles. Lara had her phone out and mouthed to her that she was live streaming.

Then Ricky blurted out, "Are you coming to live with us in New York, or are we moving here?"

"What?" Candra stopped and stared at him before turning to Monna. She held her hands over her heart because Monna was kneeling on one knee and holding out a velvet box with a diamond ring. "Will you marry me, Candra?"

She opened and closed her mouth several times before she was able to speak. "Yes." She cleared her throat. "Yes! Yes! Yes!" She fell to her knees in front of Monna. "Yes."

Monna took the ring from the box and slipped it onto Candra's finger before grabbing another box from a nearby table. It held an identical ring. With shaking hands, Candra removed the ring and slipped it onto Monna's finger.

"I love you." They both said it at once, which made Lara and Ricky laugh.

As they kissed, they heard Lara quietly talking to the live stream viewers. "That's it. Party later tonight. VIP guests will be notified of time and location. Everyone else, wait for the live stream. See you tonight."

Chapter 10

The Engagement Party

Candra had no control over what happened next. A team of people came out of nowhere and gave her a makeover. In no time, she had perfect nails, hair, and makeup. She didn't recognize herself in the mirror.

"That can't be what I look like," she said. "I've never looked like this."

"You're beautiful," Monna said. "I have something special for you to wear. It's in the bathroom."

Candra shook as she opened the door to see what awaited her. "This is happening too fast," she whispered. "What am I doing?" When she saw the outfit hanging, she knew her coworkers had made it. It had black pants with silver rhinestones, a simple black tank top, but there was a shimmering silver short sleeved mesh tunic over everything. The tunic flared at the waist creating the look of a skirt. A black belt accented with silver brought it all together, but she didn't know if it belonged under or over the tunic. She set it aside as she looked at a collection of silver jewelry. She put on the black velvet choker and a silver necklace with her initial that hung just at the hollow of her neck. Finally, she put on a deceptively simple looking diamond bracelet, or she tried to put it on.

"Let me help with that." Monna took the bracelet and deftly hooked it on her right wrist.

"I was never good with jewelry," Candra said.

"Don't worry. I will always help." Monna grabbed the belt, wrapped it around Candra's hips, and buckled it. It sat below the waistband of the pants, resting on her hips, under the tunic. She grabbed black ankle boots that Candra hadn't seen and slipped them on her feet before standing and looking into Candra's eyes. "You're beautiful."

"You already said that." Candra took a good look at Monna. She was dressed the same except in black and gold with her initial hanging around her neck. "You're beautiful too."

* * *

Monna's security team was doubled for the night. After being escorted through lesser used hallways, they left the hotel with a police escort.

In the car, Candra asked, "Is this normal?" She watched as police cars surrounded theirs before they exited the parking garage.

"No, it's not normal." Monna leaned forward to speak with the driver. "Did something happen?"

The man in the passenger seat pushed her back. "Stay back. We're using decoys. It's best if no one sees you."

"What happened?" Monna asked again.

"You received death threats after the live stream. We're bringing in more security and using local police." He checked his phone. "The location isn't secure yet. Follow the police escort," he told the driver. "They know the area."

"My children?" Monna asked.

Candra grabbed her hand and squeezed, waiting for an answer.

"Ricky and Lara arrived before the threats came in. They are being held in a safe location."

Candra felt Monna relax, but she had to ask, "Shouldn't we call off the party?"

"No," Monna said. "We can't let them control us. If I canceled every show or appearance when I was threatened, I would never leave home. We have to live our lives."

By the time they reached the party location, the security team had doubled again, making it four times the normal amount of protection.

* * *

Monna and Candra entered the building through a freight elevator. They were surrounded by security and police. Rather than going to the party, they were taken to a small office where Ricky and Lara waited for them. Candra smiled when each of them hugged her as well as Monna.

The head of security handed earpieces to each of them. Monna helped Candra put it on her ear. "We need to stay informed," she said. "We won't hear everything, but they need to have instant communication if something happens. Don't remove this. Understand?"

Candra nodded. "Of course."

"They have inspected the whole building," Lara said. "It's safe. They are performing thorough checks on everyone trying to get in. It's better security than the president."

"Ought to be," one of the police officers said. "You're the closest this country has to a royal family. Why would anyone want to hurt you?"

"That's what I want to know," Monna said. "I need to see the threats. Where's the video?"

"You don't want to see it." The head of security tried to block the computer. "Trust me."

"I do trust you, Richard, but I need to know firsthand what I'm facing." Monna pushed him aside and sat at the desk. Holding the headphones to one ear, she waited for him to play the video. She watched silently, and let the headphones fall to the floor when it finished. Her face was red as she sat breathing hard.

Candra knelt beside her and grabbed her hand. "Slow your breathing or you'll be sick." Monna didn't seem to hear her at all. Candra turned the chair until they were facing each other, reached up and took Monna's face in her hands, and kissed her. It took a few kisses before Monna responded and kissed her back.

"I love you," Candra said. "We will get through this together."

Monna nodded. "I can handle it when they threaten me, but they threatened you, Lara, and Ricky. I won't let you know what they said they want to do."

Candra held her face and stared into her eyes. "I know you're scared for your family. Fear doesn't help. You need to get angry."

Monna leaned forward until their foreheads touched. "Where did you learn that?"

Candra smiled. "I heard you say it in an interview once. It stuck with me."

* * *

Monna and Candra stood in front of a bright red door. Both were shaking. "No matter what happens," Monna said. "Remember that I love you." She threaded her fingers through Candra's and squeezed. "I'm going to talk to our guests, then we can relax and celebrate." She raised Candra's hand to her lips and kissed it but didn't let go. "Ready?"

Candra nodded.

When the door opened, they stepped out to see a small crowd of people, including all of Candra's friends from work. Lara and Ricky stood at the front. Lara was recording on her phone.

The crowd was chanting something, and it took a moment for Candra to understand. They were saying "kiss" over and over. She suspected that Ricky started it, but it didn't really matter. They had to oblige them. Monna must have reached the same conclusion because Candra found herself bent backwards in a dramatic kiss.

The crowd cheered.

Once it was quiet, Monna pulled out a microphone and addressed them. "I apologize for what you've endured tonight. It was never my intention to have everyone searched and checked against IDs. You see, we received death threats today. I say 'we' because the threats are not only for myself. My family was threatened as well. These cowards didn't even identify themselves."

Gasps spread through the crowd.

"As you know, I don't tolerate bigotry. I look out at all you, and I see people from different cultures and backgrounds. Some of you are straight, and some are gay. We all deserve to live our lives. I want to live my life with my family. What we do doesn't affect anyone but us." The crowd shouted their agreement.

"This beautiful woman," she put her arm around Candra. "This beautiful woman captured my heart, and I want to share her with the world. But haters have accused us of forcing our sinful lifestyle on the world." She stopped, and Candra reached up and wiped tears off Monna's cheek.

After a long silent moment, Monna continued. "We have been accused of spreading the sin of love, and because of that, people want to end our lives. They call our love a disease that needs to be eradicated. But hate is the real disease, and it's spreading faster than love.

"Earlier today, I was advised to cancel plans. It was even suggested that I cancel my upcoming tour." The crowd gasped. "I refuse to cancel anything. As soon as I cancel, they will have won. This is a battle I refuse to lose. So, I apologize for increased security. I hope we can still have a good time tonight."

The crowd cheered. "Now for those who don't know her, this is my fiancée, Candra." She handed the microphone to Ricky before turning back to Candra. "Ready?" she whispered.

"Yes," Candra whispered before Monna pulled her close. For a moment they stared into each other's eyes and breathed in each other's breath. Time stood still until Candra made the first move and kissed Monna. They melted into each other's embrace as the crowd cheered.

The lights dimmed as someone tapped out a rhythm on a drum. It wasn't a drum you'd hear in a band. Rather, it was a single drum. After a while a second drummer joined. Then Candra heard what sounded like a tambourine before someone began playing a flute. "What is going on?" She looked at Monna. "Did you plan this?" Monna shook her head and pointed to the dance floor.

The crowd parted and a belly dancer appeared. She wore a bright rainbow-colored flowing skirt with a belt of silver and gold bells around her hips. Her crop top was gold and silver. She carried a rainbow scarf in her hands as she danced towards them. In one smooth movement, she tossed the scarf around Candra and used it to pull her out to the dance floor.

Candra looked back at Monna and saw that she was being pulled onto the dance floor by a second belly dancer. Monna was dancing along as she tied the scarf around her hips. When she felt hands on her hips, Candra looked back at the first dancer. She had tied the scarf around her hips. "The scarf will accentuate your hips." She moved her hips in time with the music and guided Candra to move the same.

Candra felt her face get hot. "I can't move like that."

"Sure, you can," Monna said from behind her. "Watch them and follow their movements like you're looking in a mirror. I'll help."

The two dancers faced them as the crowd formed a circle around them. They moved slowly to the music. Candra tried to copy them but started laughing when she stumbled. She felt Monna place her hands on her hips. With the soft touch moving her in time with the music, she began to dance. After a few minutes she began moving her arms. The belly dancers moved faster and faster around them. The crowd cheered and clapped in time to the music. In the center of it all, Monna twirled Candra around to face her. They danced slowly in each other's arms until Candra nodded, and they danced faster until the music stopped. They collapsed into each other's arms, gasping to catch their breath. "That was fun," Candra said once she wasn't panting.

"More?" Monna asked.

"Yes, please."

* * *

Hours later, as the party was winding down, Candra saw someone she knew hadn't been there all night. She would have remembered the blonde woman wearing a t-shirt and long kilt with chunky black boots. She grabbed Monna and pointed. "Where did she come from? She looks like you from ten years ago."

"Don't let security get her." The quiet, female voice was in Candra's head. "She's not a threat. I sent her to help, but I can't keep her here long. Her name is Maddie."

Candra grabbed Monna and hurried to get to the woman before security saw her.

"Candra?" Monna tried to pull her back.

When it looked like security would reach her first, Candra yelled, "Maddie!"

Maddie looked straight into Monna's eyes. Monna gasped. "How?"

As security grabbed her, Maddie shouted, "Mother is worried. This place is bad. She's trying to fix it. Not this town. This world is bad. You need to come to the island. It's better there."

"Where? How?" Candra asked. She was pulled back by security along with Monna. "You don't understand. She's here to help."

Monna kept eye contact until the moment Maddie vanished.

All around people looked confused. It was as if it never happened, and no one knew why security was holding Monna and Candra. Candra and Monna shared a look. They both remembered Maddie.

* * *

After a long and stressful car ride back to the hotel, it was nice to relax. It was strange to have the security team stay inside the room. Candra guessed it was necessary, but privacy would have been nice.

"They will stay in the outer rooms," Monna said. "I promise." She pulled Candra down onto the bed. "We need to rest."

"And talk," Candra said as she kicked off her boots.

Monna propped her head up with pillows and pulled Candra to her side. "How did you know her name?"

"There was a voice in my head." Candra played with the necklace around Monna's neck. "I want to know who Mother is. Why did Maddie mention her? Is she the voice in my head?"

"I don't know, Baby."

Candra looked up into her eyes. "Baby?"

"You don't like it?" Monna smiled. "I can call you something else."

"I didn't say I didn't like it. It just caught me by surprise." She leaned up and kissed Monna. "I don't know what to call you now."

The soft click of the door opening made them both turn. It was one of the security men. "James," Monna said. "You need to stay in the outer room so you can protect the children too. We're fine in here alone."

"No." The voice was in Candra's head again. "I can't stop him. You need to be smart. The children are safe. I was able to get them to safety, but my power here is fading. Be careful." Candra shared a look with Monna and knew she had heard the voice this time.

"If you follow instructions, the kids will be safe." He waited for a man she didn't know to bring in a camera on a tripod. "You're going to tell the world you're wrong. You are not going to marry a woman." He grabbed Monna's arm and yanked her off the bed. She landed on her knees, and he laughed. "Stand in front of the camera like a good girl and read the cards that my friend here made for you."

While James and his friend were focused on Monna, Candra hit a button on her earpiece that she never took off. She prayed that someone would be listening. She wasn't even sure it worked that way, but she had to try. Glancing out the door, she only saw what appeared to be someone lying on the floor. She hoped he wasn't dead.

"I don't hear her reading the cards." The voice came from the outer room, and upon hearing it, all the color drained from Monna's face.

"Harvey," Monna said. "I should have known."

"You shouldn't have fired me," he said, walking through the door. "I see you still have that bitch in your bed. Should've thought about her before you punched me."

Candra's skin crawled when he looked at her.

"Now read the cards like a good girl and give me those diamond rings. I can get a pretty penny for them." He gave her a crooked smile.

"You don't care if I'm with a woman. You were always the first to suggest it for videos, even though that wasn't part of your job." Monna stood tall and refused to back away when he got close.

"But it was so easy to stir up trouble, especially in this backwards little town. It grew on its own. I just had to light the fire. Believe me. Those death threats are real, but you can stop them by reading the cards. You have to act like you mean it though. People aren't stupid."

"What happens after?" Monna asked. "We'll still be together. Nothing changes."

Harvey laughed, but James answered. "No." He pointed at Candra. "She comes with us, and you get to keep your children safe."

"Never gonna happen," Candra said.

"You would sacrifice your children to stay with her?" James asked.

"No." Monna said. "But I will sacrifice both of you." She looked Harvey in the eyes. "You always underestimated me. No more." She kicked the closest leg of the tripod, sending it crashing to the floor. Pieces of the camera flew in all directions. "Wow! Cheap camera."

Harvey pulled out his phone. "We can still do this."

"Uh, Guys, I wouldn't do that." It was the man who had brought in the camera, and he was surrounded by at least a dozen police officers, all with guns drawn.

Monna's head of security ran past him into the room and pulled Candra and Monna out of the way. "I heard everything when you changed the channel on your earpiece. How did you know to do that?"

"I didn't know what else to try," Candra said. "It was a shot in the dark."

"Lara and Ricky are safe in another hotel. We'll get you there as soon as we can." He smiled at Monna. "You got yourself a smart girl here. Don't do anything to lose her."

Chapter 11

Wedding Plans

"I don't know how this world got so bad. I tried to fix it, but I had to ask for help. You are much better at these things. I should just stop trying."

"This one wasn't your fault, Dear," Mother said. "I have warned you to call me sooner when a ripple is out of control, but this happened more quickly than even I expected."

"Did it bleed into the others?" the male voice asked.

"No, but it created several more toxic worlds. I was forced to destroy them entirely."

He heard the pain in her voice. "Your children? What about them?"

Her voice shook as she answered. "I couldn't spare the time to save them."

"I'm sorry, Dear. How do we save this one?"

"I'm afraid we can't. The plague of hatred makes it difficult for me to use my magic. We need to work together if we want to save my children and grandchildren."

"Candra, Dear? Her too?"

"Yes, she's family now."

* * *

Candra looked at sketches of dresses with one of the designers at her job. "I don't even know if this will happen. The world wants to stop us, Scott. We just want to be happy."

Scott hugged her. "Monna is right though. You can't let them dictate your life." He turned the virtual page on the computer screen and pointed to a sketch. "This is my favorite. You would look wonderful in this."

Candra touched the screen. "It's not white. Shouldn't it be white?"

He smiled. "Nothing about this wedding is traditional. Why should the dress be any different? I happen to know Monna loves the way you look in pink."

"But it's so bright."

Candra jumped when a loud alarm blared at the front door. Security rushed to meet the threat, but it was Brent, the other designer. "Sorry. Sorry," he said, holding up his hands. "I forgot about the metal detectors. I have zippers, chains, buckles, and buttons." He submitted to a search.

Monna joined them from down the hallway. "Thanks, Richard. Good to know my head of security is on top of things." She winked at Candra.

"Is that sarcasm?" Richard asked.

Monna didn't answer as she took Brent by the arm and led him to his office. She winked once more before disappearing into the office.

Candra followed Scott back to his office. "They're using zippers, chains, and buckles. I can't stand not knowing what she'll be wearing."

"She's tried to peek at my sketches, but I've managed to keep them hidden from her," Scott said.

"I want to go with the pink, but I want silver accents. Can we do that?" Candra stared at the sketch. "What fabrics will you use?"

Scott grabbed a roll of fabric that was propped up in the corner. "I knew you would go with the pink. I bought some silk for it."

"Real silk?" Candra asked as she ran her hand over the fabric.

"Of course. Real silk," Scott said. "And these." He handed her a package of buttons.

"Rainbow buttons!" She threw her arms around his neck. "You think of everything!"

"Can I have complete control over the design? Do you trust me?" He asked.

"Absolutely!"

* * *

Monna never watched the news and never viewed social media. Lara posted everything for her. After the engagement party and accompanying death threats, Candra followed her lead and ignored it all. Everyone around them knew not to mention anything they saw or heard.

Security was a nightmare as they rushed preparations for the wedding. Monna wanted it to happen before her tour started. Candra wondered if the tour would actually happen. At least getting the marriage license was uneventful. The security at the county courthouse was almost as good as Monna's personal security. The security team waited in the lobby while only Richard went inside with them.

"That was too easy," Richard said once they were back at the hotel. "I don't like it."

"There was an anonymous tip that you were going to a different courthouse to get the license," Lara said.

"You?" Monna asked.

Lara shook her head.

Candra wondered aloud, "Maddie?"

Monna shrugged. "Maybe. Or the voice."

"Well, whoever it was, we have an ally." Candra dropped onto the sofa and pulled Monna down with her. "I think we deserve to relax a little."

Richard cleared his throat. "I have news." They both stared at him waiting. "We were able to secure your first-choice location for the wedding, but it's only for this Saturday. I'm told the dresses will be finished in time. With the limited guest list, it should be easy to hide it."

"Let's hope our anonymous helper can distract the haters," Monna said.

"I wouldn't count on it," Richard said.

"Maybe we should pray," Candra said.

* * *

Traditionally, the couple to be married doesn't see each other the day of the wedding until the actual ceremony, but nothing about this wedding was traditional. So, Candra and Monna rode together in the same car to an undisclosed location.

When Richard joined them, he said, "The location changed. I'm sorry." He waited until the car door opened and a familiar person scooted in next to Monna. "I believe you know Maddie."

As the car started moving, Maddie spoke, but it was clear that it wasn't just her. "We don't have much time. I've found a way to share Maddie's body for a time so I can help you. I will officiate the ceremony. Afterwards, you and your guests will be taken to another world where it's safe. Then I must destroy this place before the hate spreads. I can't tolerate so much hate."

"Who are you?" Monna asked, staring into Maddie's eyes. "What's your name?"

She kissed Monna's forehead. "I'm your mother."

A tear rolled down Monna's cheek. "But you died."

"When you were a child. Yes, but I've been watching over you all these years. I'm proud of you. You're strong, but you can't win against this hatred. It's grown too strong."

"Where are we going?" Candra asked.

"I have prepared a place full of magic with the help of my husband. He's losing his mind a little, but he knows how to use magic. Most importantly, he knows what will happen if we fail today."

Candra wiped tears from Monna's cheeks. "Things will be okay. That's all we wanted."

"We're almost there," Richard said.

Monna looked out the window and shook her head. "This doesn't look right. Where are we? I see palm trees."

"Magic." It sounded more like Maddie that time. "The cars travel farther than just on the road."

"Is that an island?" Candra asked

"It is," Mother said. "We're still in your world with a chance of being found. I need the love generated at the wedding to power the magic."

"I don't understand." Monna slowly climbed out of the car with Maddie and Candra. "How will this work?"

"Don't try to understand. Just let it happen. It's easier."

"Thanks, Maddie," Candra said.

The next half hour was a blur. Candra and Monna were taken into separate outdoor tents to change clothes and have their hair and makeup done. When the music started, Ricky came to get her to escort her down the aisle.

Her breath caught in her throat when she saw Monna standing with Maddie, but she laughed when she realized Maddie was still wearing the same t-shirt and long kilt. It didn't matter though, Monna's dress was the most beautiful she'd ever seen.

Monna was dressed in a slinky white dress with black and gold pinstripes. It was cinched at the waist with a corset using gold buckles. Her eyes lit up when she saw Candra in her pink silk dress with its layers of rainbow chiffon under the full skirt. When she saw the rainbow buttons down the back of the dress, Monna laughed.

It didn't stay nice for long. As they kissed at the end, the cheers from the guests were drowned out by the sound of helicopters overhead.

"They found us!" Candra shouted.

"Mother!" Monna turned to Maddie for help.

Maddie glowed as a booming male voice drowned out the sound of the helicopters. "No one move! Everyone on the ground is safe. Close your eyes and count to ten before you open them."

Candra and Monna counted together. "One. Two. Three." The ground shook. "Four. Five. Six." They could see the glow even with their eyes closed. "Seven. Eight. Nine. Ten." They felt like they were enveloped in a warm embrace, and they opened their eyes.

They were inside a diner, and the people inside were disturbingly familiar. Maddie was no longer beside them. She was with the group across the diner.

Mother spoke to them. "This is your home now, Monna. Your wedding guests are outside. These are your counterparts from my other worlds. You are all safe here. When the glow fades, they will see you. It would be helpful if you told them who I am so I can talk to them. Understand?"

Monna nodded. When the glow faded, she heard Maddie ask if the voice was their mother. "She is our mother." Monna said.

Mother launched into her heartfelt speech for all to hear. Afterwards, she faded away, but they all still felt her.

Eddie brought breakfast and coffee as Candra began telling the tale of her adventure with Monna.

Chapter 12

Maddie's Wild Adventure

Maybe it was the timing of when she appeared or possibly how she was created, but Maddie heard the voices more clearly than the others. She wasn't always the fragile one. She survived two divorces and became stronger because of that. It wasn't until she heard the first voice that the trouble started, but the voice wasn't meant for her. Being created out of chaos didn't help.

Emma performed the final song of the show and was rushed to the waiting car as usual. Unknown to her, in another universe Donna was being summoned by a senile magic user, but he was distracted. He moved the wrong vehicle in the wrong universe. As Emma's car crossed the bridge into town, she was duplicated.

"I'm sorry," her driver said. "I don't know how we got here. I don't know where we are."

"I do. Just follow the road into town. I'll explain later," Emma said. She looked into her own eyes. "You would be Six. I hate that everyone calls you by numbers. Do you want to pick a new name?"

"Someone called us Maddie once. I like that name." She tugged at the hem of her white t-shirt. "Can I use it?"

Emma placed her hand on Maddie's to stop her fidgeting. "I like it. From now on, you will be Maddie." She looked up to see the diner. "Stop here," she told the driver. "Maddie, you have my memories. You know what happens now."

"Yes." She leaned close as they kissed each other's cheeks. As she scooted out of the car, Emma slapped her ass. She turned and stared. There was something different about her eyes, and she didn't think it was Emma anymore.

* * *

Maddie entered the diner right before closing time. "I'm not here for food," she said to the young man trying to shoo her out. She pointed to the table in the corner. "I need to see them."

"Oh, Emma. It's you." He smiled. "I thought you were on tour."

"Emma is on tour. I'm Maddie." On seeing his blank stare, she said, "I'm confused too. I don't know why I'm here."

Two through Five didn't acknowledge her as she pulled up a chair to join them. The appearance of a new version of themselves was nothing new. She knew what they were doing. Emma had them watching performance videos and looking for places for improvement.

Maddie had no interest in doing that. She wanted to be her own person. She needed to be separate from them. After several awkward minutes, she stood. That's when she saw Dawn sitting alone in the corner. Maddie knew she was shy, but she took a chance and walked over.

"Hi, may I sit? You're Dawn, right?" She fussed with the hem of her shirt.

Dawn looked up. "You're not like the others." She waved at the seat with a shaking hand. "Is she here?"

"Who?" Maddie tucked her skirt under her as she sat. "Emma? She was brought here by … Well, I don't know how. She was leaving the show, and then we were on the bridge. She brought me here and left." Maddie stared down at her hands on the table. "I don't know what to do here. I want to go back and help Emma."

"Rest first," Dawn said. "Gather your energy." Dawn stood. "I need to go. It's much later than I thought it was."

"I need a place to stay." Maddie stood and smoothed her skirt. "Where do I go? I can't ask them."

"Come with me. I know a place."

* * *

Maddie stayed in a room in the house next to the diner. She was on the second floor with Dawn. The third floor was occupied by Two through Five, and Dawn said Emma stayed there when she was in town.

After a few weeks without hearing from Emma, Maddie started pacing up and down the hallway every day. Dawn bumped into her one day. "You will ruin the floor if you keep doing that."

"I can't stay here, Dawn." Her skirt swirled around her legs as she turned to walk back the other direction. "I miss performing. I miss the cheering crowds. I miss being Emma, but I want to be me too."

"That's not how this place works," Dawn said.

Maddie stopped in front of her. "I know, but those four ... I can't take being around them anymore. I can't live that life. I need to be me, and that can't happen here."

* * *

Maddie was well on her way to the bridge when she heard the voice. "You need a car." The male voice was loud in her head. It felt like sandpaper in her mind. She ignored it and kept walking. "The magic won't let you leave without a car. The metal makes it work." She continued on her path. "You can take a car from the auto shop. He has cars from people who disappeared. He left the keys in one of them. You can take it."

"It would make it easier," Maddie said. After a short walk back to town, she found the car with little trouble. It was an older black car with chrome trim. It had been years since she drove a car, but she was willing to try.

In no time she was driving across the bridge, but she slammed on the brakes when she saw a police car farther up the road. What if they stopped her?

Then she saw the man. He was standing on the side of the road. He stared at her as the world went dark. After a few seconds she could see again. She pounded on her window. "Help me! I'm trapped in this crazy car!" The man approached the car, but before he reached her, the world went black again.

Maddie felt the car moving with her foot still on the brake. "I guess I'm not in control anymore." She grabbed the steering wheel with both hands and said a silent thanks that she remembered to buckle the seatbelt. When the light returned she saw a woman walking in the middle of a city street. No one else was around. In a panic, she turned the steering wheel to swerve around the woman. Her heart skipped a beat and she couldn't breathe when she saw it was Emma. She repeatedly pushed the brake pedal, but the car didn't stop.

Everything changed again as lightning lit the sky followed by a loud boom of thunder. Rain poured down all around. She drove through puddles inches deep. In the rearview mirror, she saw Emma still walking and tried to turn around. The steering didn't respond.

"What the hell is going on here?"

The sky lit with multiple bolts of lightning. When they stopped, the sun was out. She tried again to stop the car. "Seriously! What is happening?" She held the wheel and prayed she didn't crash as the car drove itself in circles past the same building. Eventually, she drove past a crowd of people straight towards Emma. "Move! I can't stop!" She wanted to close her eyes, but she had to see too. At the last second, someone pulled Emma out of the way.

Immediately, she felt the rumble of the car going across the bridge, and the world went dark. She closed her eyes and waited for a crash, but the car stopped before hitting anything. When she opened her eyes, she saw the man standing inches in front of the car. He looked older, but it was him.

He walked to the car and opened the door, but he couldn't get her to release the steering wheel. "Six," he said. "Emma has been worried sick about you."

She didn't look at him. "Maddie."

"What?" he asked.

"My name." She finally looked at him. "I like to be called Maddie." She let go of the wheel and fell into his arms.

He unbuckled her seatbelt and lifted her from the car. They talked as he helped her sit on a rock nearby. She knew she didn't make much sense talking about her harrowing drive, and she laughed when he checked her head for an injury. "I didn't hit my head."

He looked her over more, and once convinced she wasn't injured, he introduced himself. "I'm John. I run the auto repair shop across from the diner. How do you feel?"

She smiled at him. "I'm hungry. What time is it? Is the diner still open?" She stood and twirled around, making her skirt fly up, revealing shorts underneath. "I'm fine. I'm just famished."

"Of course, the diner's open," he said. "It's open twenty-four hours."

Maddie grabbed his arm. "Since when?"

He shrugged. "I guess it was a few years back when Dawn put in the stage and karaoke machine."

She tugged on her t-shirt. "Dawn owns the diner? When did that happen? How long have I been gone, John?"

They left the car behind and walked to town. "How long have I been gone, John?"

He paused a little too long. "It's been ten years, Maddie."

He let her walk in silence to the diner where Emma pulled her into a hug. She had to study Emma's face and eyes closely. She was older, but it was definitely Emma.

104

Maddie learned that the others except for Dawn had disappeared.

"I'm happy you didn't disappear," Emma said.

The world turned black yet again, and she almost lost her balance when the light returned. She was standing on top of the car with another car coming towards her. She threw her hands up to shield her eyes from the headlights as the car stopped.

She watched as someone who looked like Emma got out with another woman. They were holding hands. "What's going on here? Who are you?"

Maddie slid down the windshield and hopped to the ground, fixing her skirt that had ridden up. "People call me Six in my world, but I prefer the name Maddie."

"Your world?" both women asked.

Maddie nodded. "It's hard to explain." She paused and played with the hem of her shirt. "Have you heard the voice inside your head?"

"No," the look alike said.

At the same time, her friend said, "Yes. I've heard it."

"Do you think it's God? Because I'm tired of being moved around like this. All I did was leave town. I couldn't take being around Two through Five. Dawn is nice, but she doesn't talk to anyone. Emma tried to help, but I knew more would come. So, when the voice told me to leave, I left, but it felt like I was being pulled in two directions."

After stumbling forward a bit, the friend approached Maddie. "I don't know if the voice is God or not. Every time I heard it, I found Donna." Maddie frowned, and she gestured behind her. "Because of the voice, I saved her life." She grabbed Maddie's hands and stared into her eyes. "What do you mean about your world? Where are you from?"

"The voice told me that I have to go back to my own universe. I don't belong here," Maddie said. "He was insistent about it." She looked down at the ground.

"He?" Maddie felt her finger under her chin and let her lift her face. "My voice is a woman."

Donna cleared her throat. "Can we all get in one car and go to the hotel now?"

"No!" The male voice speaking aloud made the ground shake. They stumbled into each other. "Maddie goes back to her world. You two stay here."

"Take their hands. Both of them." A quiet feminine voice was in Maddie's head. "I will deal with the loud, obnoxious one. Don't let go of each other until all of you are in the car. Drive away. Direction doesn't matter. I will get you where you need to go. Then I can fix this mess."

Maddie hurried with the others to get into the car. The driver barely waited for the doors to shut before driving away. In no time the scenery had changed, and they approached a bridge. A small group of people stood at the opposite end of the bridge.

"That's Emma and Dawn," Maddie said. "This is my home."

Maddie didn't know what to do once they all stood together near the bridge. She wanted to run to the others, but her legs felt frozen in place. John started by introducing himself, and everyone followed his lead.

Then Emma spoke directly to Maddie, and it was Emma. "I was worried about you." She held out her hands towards Maddie. "Again." Maddie rushed into her arms. "I hope we're done with this. My heart can't take anymore."

Maddie nodded. "You're like a mother to me." She squeezed her arms around Emma. "I didn't really want to go, but it was crowded, and the voice told me to go."

Maddie stayed silent as everyone talked around her, content to be in Emma's arms again. After another interruption from the loud male voice, Maddie pushed away from Emma and looked towards the sky. She was shaking. "Will I vanish again? I don't want to go."

An invisible force surrounded her in a soft glowing light as she heard the feminine voice in her head. "Maddie, you are special. I know you want to know who I am. Please call me Mother. I want you to stay and be happy with John. Dawn can stay too."

Maddie felt invisible arms wrap around her and smiled.

"I died years ago, but I took over as caretaker of the universes. There are many. Whenever anyone makes a decision, a new universe is created that takes them on a new path away from the other decisions they could have made. It's messy, but many times multiple decisions lead to the same eventual path. So those worlds merge again. But some decisions are huge and cause ripples through multiple worlds. I created a way to control those ripples by containing them here in this town. It has helped, but there are still many problems I must fix. It will take time."

As Mother spoke, Maddie saw images of all of them and the ripples created. Tears flowed down her cheeks as she felt love flood through her. "I need you to tell the others while I fix everything. Okay?" Maddie nodded. "But first, I need your help. Another world is in danger. We need to go. Time will slow here until you return. You need to find Monna and Candra. Tell them they need to come here. If you can touch them, then I can bring them here. I can't keep us there for long. Try to be quick."

Maddie closed her eyes, and when she opened them again, she was surrounded by people and loud music. It took a minute, but she saw Monna and Candra. They were trying to talk to her, but she couldn't hear. Security guards grabbed her, and she heard Candra scream her name.

Maddie shouted, "Mother is worried. This place is bad. She's trying to fix it. Not this town. This world is bad. You need to come to the island. It's better there."

Candra was close enough to hear, but security was keeping them apart. "Where? How?" Candra asked. She was pulled back by security. "You don't understand," she told the guard. "She's here to help."

Maddie reached out to Candra as she slipped into darkness. She returned to town without Mother. No one knew she was gone for several minutes. She walked with the others to the diner. It was becoming a familiar path.

She barely remembered talking with the others or watching the craziness outside. Without much warning, she told them what Mother said to her by the bridge. She thought it would comfort them, but it brought up more questions instead.

It was horrible not feeling Mother there with her, but she was unprepared for the feeling when she returned. Mother didn't surround her. Maddie felt her inside like they were sharing her body.

"We need to return and bring as many here as we can. I wish I could explain now, but we need to go now." In the time it took Maddie to blink, she was standing outside a car. The car door opened, and she scooted in next to Monna. "I believe you know Maddie," the security man in the front said.

Mother spoke as the car started moving. "We don't have much time. I've found a way to share Maddie's body for a time so I can help you. I will officiate the ceremony. Afterwards, you and your guests will be taken to another world where it's safe. Then I must destroy this place before the hate spreads. I can't tolerate so much hate."

"Who are you?" Monna asked, staring into Maddie's eyes. "What's your name?"

She kissed Monna's forehead. "I'm your mother."

Crying, Monna said, "But you died."

"When you were a child. Yes, but I've been watching over you all these years. I'm proud of you. You're strong, but you can't win against this hatred. It's grown too strong."

"Where are we going?" Candra asked.

"I have prepared a place full of magic with the help of my husband. He's losing his mind a little, but he knows how to use magic. Most importantly, he knows what will happen if we fail today."

Candra wiped tears from Monna's cheeks. "Things will be okay. That's all we wanted."

The drive to the island town was short, and the wedding ceremony happened too quickly. When she heard helicopters, Mother told her it was time to go. The male voice boomed and told everyone to close their eyes and count to ten. Maddie didn't know how it would work. There were over two hundred people. "Don't worry, Maddie. With my husband's help, we can do this, but I will need to rest afterwards."

The world went dark, the world shook, and the warm light embraced everything. Maddie was standing in the diner between Emma and Dawn. Her memory was becoming fuzzy about the engagement party and wedding. She watched with the others as Monna and Candra appeared. Monna told them the voice was their mother, and Maddie remembered that, but the rest was fading. Mother talked to them like family, and that helped.

Maddie could travel to her world from ten years ago using the bridge. She could continue her concert tour that was interrupted. That's all she wanted when she left town that day. For her it had only been a couple days. Continuing would be easy. John would join her when he could, and Mother would be there whenever she needed her. If she needed inspiration, Emma, Donna, and Monna had already lived through other albums and concert tours, but maybe she would create new music.

Chapter 13

Dawn Discovers a Glitch in the Magic

I wasn't used to having a full house. It was a big house, which had been a bed and breakfast at one time. I don't remember it actually having rooms for rent. Every now and then I considered renting rooms, but I always felt it was better to help people down on their luck by giving them a free place to sleep. After all, that's what the last owner of the house and diner did for me.

After Mother brought new arrivals from another universe, the house was full. Along with many in town, I opened my home to as many as I could. John, the mechanic, already stayed with me as it kept him close to the auto shop. Maddie moved into his room. Donna and Cassie moved in as well as Monna and Candra. Of course, Emma has her own set of rooms close to my rooms.

With five more people in the house and Emma staying here often, things were tense. It didn't help that the three couples were affectionate all the time. I've seen so many public displays of affection, I thought of locking myself in my room for a week.

Late one night, I sat at a booth in the diner eating ice cream while trying to read. The ice cream was good but not satisfying, and I'd read the same page of the book at least ten times without knowing what it said. Going up to my room was not an option unless I wanted to listen to everyone having sex again.

Don't get me wrong. I'm happy for them, but it makes me wish I had someone too.

"Maybe I should fix you up with someone."

I dropped my book. "Emma. Don't do that. I could have spilled my ice cream." She picked up my book and handed it to me before sliding into the booth next to me. She always did that. Never once has she sat across from me. "Thanks." I scooted to make more room for her.

"I'm serious, Dawn." She dipped her finger in the ice cream and licked it. "You need someone. What about that security guard you danced with when we celebrated Monna's wedding."

"No thanks." I looked through the book trying to find my lost spot.

Emma took another taste of my ice cream, using my spoon this time. "Would you prefer a woman?"

I didn't answer, and I kept my head down. I opened the book and tried to read something, but the words didn't make sense.

Emma closed the book. "It's easier to read when it's right side up." She placed her hand on top of mine. "Tell me what's wrong. Was it something I said?"

"I don't want you to set me up with someone. I have someone I like." I pulled my hand away from hers and ate some ice cream. "I just can't tell her. She wouldn't understand."

"Is it someone I know?" Emma asked.

Again, I didn't answer.

"Dawn, we talk about everything. Please, talk to me." She leaned close and put her arm around me. "I want to help you."

I felt like I had a thousand butterflies in my stomach, but I had to say something. I was trapped in the booth with her holding me tight. There was no way out. "I've never been with anyone. Never once. I dream about it all the time. I want it so much, but we can't."

"We can't?" Emma let go of my shoulders and turned her whole body to face me. "Dawn?"

I looked at her, trying to think. Words wouldn't come. She was so beautiful. I noticed she'd added red highlights to her golden hair. Shaking my head, I said, "I didn't mean that."

She took my chin in her hand and looked into my eyes. "Yes you did. Tell me what you want."

I closed my eyes. "Forget I said anything and let me leave. We can't ever do anything. If people found out I even thought about it, it would be horrible. I never should have said anything. Please let me go."

Without a word, Emma stood and let me out of the booth. I ran out of the diner and to the house next door. Once in my room, I cried myself to sleep.

* * *

In the morning, I found a note slipped under my door. I recognized Emma's handwriting and almost didn't open it, but my curiosity got the best of me. It wasn't what I expected at all.

Dawn,

I know you're frustrated. I can help if you let me. No commitment. No one but the two of us will know. I have left a gift for you outside your door. Wear it tonight. I will come by at midnight and knock three times. If you want this, open the door. Otherwise, I will leave and never speak of this again. Either way, know that I only want the best for you.

Love,
Eme

"Eme? Is that what she wants me to call her now? Not Emma?" I had a million thoughts running through my head. This couldn't be what I wanted it to be. She must have misunderstood. I opened the door and grabbed a small gift bag sitting on the floor.

Back inside my room, I peeked into the bag and felt the butterflies return. Emma knew exactly what my fantasy was. On top of the black lingerie was another note. The handwriting was different, but it was still clearly written by Emma.

When you wear this, call me Eme. This will be our secret. After tonight, Eme will be there only when you request her.

I fondled the lacy garments. "Of course, she knows my size."

All day, I wondered what Emma was doing. I didn't see her anywhere, and I started to think I had dreamed the whole thing. Finally, at dinner time, she came into the diner with the others. We all sat in the large circular corner booth. Emma sat on my right side; Maddie sat on my left.

Emma smiled at me but didn't give any indication that anything had happened. Everything was normal until she left the diner. I swear she winked at me. I felt like I couldn't breathe. Maddie stopped and checked on me. I could not explain this to her, especially when I didn't even know if I imagined it. "I'm okay," I said.

Once the others had left, I stayed as late as I dared, and headed home just after eleven. I breathed easier when I didn't see anyone. Though I did hear the couples laughing and moaning behind their doors along with the occasional squeaky bed.

Inside my room, I stared at the lingerie lying on the bed. I wasn't sure if I wanted this to happen, but I changed into it. After all, I could always ignore the knock.

I looked at myself in the mirror and didn't recognize myself. Before I had time to contemplate what would happen, I saw the clock change to twelve. I heard a single, loud knock on the door. I waited and counted. At the count of ten, I heard a second knock. I walked to the door. When I touched the doorknob, I heard and felt the third knock.

I hesitated for a count to ten. Then I opened the door. The doorknob rattled as my hand shook.

She stood before me in a black silk robe tied at the waist. I could see black fishnet stockings and black high heeled shoes and found myself wondering what she wore under the robe. Backing up, I let her inside and closed the door behind her.

When I turned back to her, she had untied her robe and let it fall to the floor. She was wearing a black leather corset and lace panties. I didn't know what to do, but she did.

"Stand still. Let me look at you."

"Yes, Eme."

She smiled at me briefly before she inspected me. She ran her hand across my shoulders and down my arm. I shivered at the soft touch. "Are you cold?"

"No, Eme."

She stepped in front of me and ran the backs of her fingers over my breasts. I gasped as the lace moved across them with her touch. "I want to be perfectly clear." She squatted and ran her palms down my legs to my bare feet. "I am here to help you. I want you to enjoy everything." She stood and gazed into my eyes. "If, at any time, you want me to leave, call me Emma and tell me to stop. Do you understand?"

"Yes, Eme."

We stood gazing into each other's eyes for a long time before she grabbed the back of my neck and pulled me close. I wasn't prepared for the feel of her tongue against my lips, and I gasped. Her soft lips pressed against mine as she kissed me. My legs were weak, and I didn't know how I was still standing.

When she pulled back, she walked around and stopped behind me. I was breathing so fast. I didn't know what to expect. I could feel her lean against me. Her breath was hot on my shoulders. I waited, but she didn't do anything.

"Please, Eme," I said when I couldn't wait any longer. "Please, touch me. I need you."

I was rewarded as she wrapped both arms around my waist and pulled me against her. Her left hand held me tight while her right hand moved down and lifted the waist of my lace panties. "Do you like this?"

"Yes, Eme."

"I know you want more." Her lips touched my ear as she talked to me. When she kissed my ear, I lost my balance. She laughed as we toppled over onto the bed.

I found myself lying on my back with her kneeling between my legs. She kicked off her shoes. I waited as she unhooked her corset and tossed it on the floor. The bra she wore was sheer. I shouldn't have been surprised at how she looked. After all, we basically have the same body, but I was in a trance watching her crawl over me. After a brief kiss to my lips, she trailed kisses down my chin and neck.

She rolled to the side and ran her hand down my stomach and slipped her fingers inside the lace panties. I gasped when she didn't stop where I expected.

"I want you to move your hips. Rock them up and down. Move the way you do when you dance." Her voice sent another shiver through me. I moved my hips a little. "You can do better than that." She started to sing. I knew the song. I've danced to it. "Move to the music." She sang again as she moved her hand against me. It was all a dance. I moved faster, pushing against her hand. I sang along with her. When it almost became too much, I finally crashed over the edge in waves of pleasure.

I wrapped my arms around her and pulled her close as I kissed her. Her lips were soft against mine, and I wanted more. I moved my hand against her skin as I wondered what to do for her, but she pushed away.

"Not today," she said. "I'm here for you, not me." She kissed my cheek, and suddenly she was Emma, not Eme.

"But?" I reached for her as she stood.

"I'm fine." She picked up her corset and robe and slipped on her shoes. "Sleep now. I know you need it."

As she left my room, I cried, but I didn't know if it was for me or for her.

* * *

I walked into the diner and saw the three couples sitting in the large booth in the corner. Maddie waved at me to join them. I wanted to find Emma, but the food did look good. Eddie always brought us family style meals.

As I filled a plate and poured some coffee, Maddie touched my arm. "Are you okay, Dawn?" she whispered in my ear. "I thought I heard you crying last night."

I wanted to lie, but the concern in her voice made me think of Mother. "I don't know, Maddie. Everything was fine until ..." I couldn't tell her.

"Someone was in your room, and they left too soon?" she asked. "I heard the knocks at midnight."

"I didn't know you were dating anyone."

I don't know who said that, but now everyone was looking at me. "I'm not dating anyone. It was a one-time thing, and it ended too soon. That's all. I'm fine. Really."

No one spoke, but I felt their eyes on me. Then I heard Mother's voice in my head. "I need to talk to you. Go somewhere you won't be disturbed." I stood, nearly knocking over my coffee. "I just remembered I need to do something that can't wait."

As I rushed out the door, I ran into Emma. She grabbed my shoulders to keep me from falling. My heart skipped a beat. "Emma." She shook her head. "Eme?" She nodded.

"We didn't finish last night," she said.

I felt her grip on my shoulders tighten as she pulled me towards her. "I can't do anything right now."

"Let me help," Mother's voice said before I felt us pulled away from each other by invisible hands. "Go somewhere she won't think to look so we can talk."

"Sorry, Emma. I have to go." I didn't look back as I ran out the door.

I circled around to the back of the diner and went back inside. Eddie was surprised to see me, but he promised he wouldn't say anything to the others as I took the stairs down to the wine cellar. It was huge with plenty of places to hide.

"I'm ready to talk." I felt funny talking to no one, but Mother responded in my head.

"Dawn, Emma tried to duplicate herself again, but it didn't work the way it should have."

I sighed. "Oh. That's what you want to talk about. I thought you were angry about what we did last night. It won't happen again." I walked along the rows of wine bottles, but I stopped when I heard her response.

"It needs to happen again, but it must be with Emma. Not Eme."

I looked around as if I might see Mother somewhere. "I don't understand. Why?"

"Emma wanted to help you, but she needs to help herself too. She tried to use the magic, but it's too weak after bringing so many people here. Eme should have become a duplicate, but she remained inside Emma's head." I felt a buzzing in my head as Mother paused. "I think Eme is trying to break free. I don't have the strength to fix it if it happens. I need you to help Emma realize that Eme needs to remain a part of her."

I threw up my hands. "How am I supposed to do that? Huh?" Mother didn't answer. "Last night, Emma appeared to me when I showed love and concern for her. I thought it was role play, and I thought she broke character."

"No," Mother said. "She split herself. You need to help her heal herself. She can't do it alone."

"Will I disappear?" I had wondered this since the day Two disappeared. "I don't want to die."

"I don't know, Dawn." I felt a warm caress all over. "I love you. I want nothing more than for you to stay. Emma needs you this way. Maddie needs your friendship too. I will try my best to keep you here, but I'm still weak. Try to find something to ground you here. It may help."

I nod and smile even though tears are rolling down my cheeks. "What happens to me if I disappear?" I wasn't sure I was ready for the answer, but I needed to know.

"I will bring you to live with me. I have others here from the worlds I couldn't save. You will have a place. I promise. I love my children and want the best for all of you. I will fight with all my strength to save you and Emma. Now. Dry your tears and find Emma before it's too late."

* * *

120

I entered the diner through the kitchen. I heard a crowd of people talking as they ate breakfast. The diner was full of people from town, and Emma sat with Maddie in the corner. The others were not there.

Emma looked up when I entered the room, and I wondered if she could feel my presence. I watched her as I walked towards their booth. The moment I was within arm's reach, her expression changed. I knew it was Eme and stepped back. I watched her eyes. They changed when I stepped back. I didn't know how I was going to do this.

"Dawn, are you okay?" Emma asked.

"You didn't finish your breakfast earlier," Maddie said.

I smiled and waved my hand. "I'm fine."

Emma stood and took my arm. "You need to eat." The touch and voice were clearly Eme once more. She pulled me to the booth and waited for me to sit before sitting so close we were touching.

I was trapped between Eme and Maddie. "Really. I'm okay."

Maddie poured fresh coffee. "At least have some coffee."

I wrapped my hands around the warm mug and took slow sips as I waited. Sooner or later Eme would do something. I felt her eyes on me, but I didn't look at her. Giving her attention would only encourage her. "Thank you, Maddie. Coffee is just what I needed this morning." I could tell Eme wasn't happy about my conversation with Maddie. I expected a response right away and was rewarded with an impatient question.

"What are your plans today?" Eme asked as she put her hand on my leg. "We have unfinished business." She moved her hand up my leg. "We were interrupted last night."

I ignored her and sipped my coffee. It had the desired effect. Eme grabbed the coffee and set it down before she turned my face to meet her gaze.

"Emma, what is wrong with you?" I heard the worry in Maddie's voice, and I hoped Mother was speaking to her.

"She's not Emma," I told her. "Isn't that right? Eme."

Eme squeezed my thigh as she ran her other hand through my hair. "Either we go home now, or I will continue our business here for all to see." She grabbed the back of my head and pulled me closer. "It doesn't matter to me where we do this."

I nodded my head as much as I could. "Maddie, we will be leaving now." I slipped a note into Maddie's hand. "Here's that information I promised you earlier." I hoped she understood. I had no way to know if Mother told her anything. The note was my only way to have her ready to help if I needed it.

As Eme pulled me out of the booth, I heard Maddie say. "I will see you later. I promise."

What was normally a short walk home to my house next door felt like an eternity. Eme held my arm the whole time. I couldn't get away from her even if I wanted to.

Once in my room with the door shut, Eme pulled me close and slipped her knee between my legs. She was so close that I felt her breath on my face. It took everything in me, but I didn't react.

"I wasn't finished with you last night. You have more to learn." She kissed my neck as she rubbed her body against mine.

I focused on keeping my breathing slow and steady. "Last night wasn't about learning. It was about frustration, stress, and finding relief." I took a deep breath and released it as she reached up to unbutton my shirt. "I just needed to get laid. I'm okay now. You can leave." I grabbed her hands and pushed her away.

"No." It was still Eme. I was too close to her. "I think you need a different lesson now."

Before I knew what happened, Eme grabbed me and pulled me face down across her lap as she sat on the bed. Instantly, I regretted wearing a skirt. She lifted it and smacked my ass. I cried out.

Before she could slap me again, invisible hands lifted me to my feet. "Hurry to the bathroom," Mother said inside my head. "Close and lock the door.

I didn't hesitate. Once inside the bathroom, I sank to the floor. "What now?"

"Dawn? How did I get here? Are you okay? Please talk to me." It was Emma, but I didn't dare open the door.

"Emma, we have a huge problem."

* * *

Emma listened as Mother and I explained the situation with Eme. She was silent a long time before she responded. "So, the plan is for you to guide me through sex, but if we see each other or touch each other …"

"Eme appears and you're lost again." I moved to sit cross-legged facing the door. "I think the best way would be to force Eme to observe, but we can't allow her to participate."

Emma made some strange noises on the other side of the door. "I have an idea, but I need Maddie's help. I need to get her."

Right on time, Maddie knocked on the door. I listened to whispering and more strange noises. "She's ready," Maddie said. "I will be in the hallway with John. He has a taser, just in case. I hope Mother can keep Emma here long enough."

"You can open the door and see her." Mother's voice was too quiet, and I wondered if she was embarrassed. I know I was. When I didn't move, Mother's invisible hands lifted me and unlocked the door. "I will help as much as I can. Don't be embarrassed. I have observed worse things than this. Remember how much you love her. It will strengthen you."

Before Mother could push me, I opened the door. Emma was leaning against pillows on the bed, wearing only her bra and panties. Her left hand was tied to the bed above her head. Her right hand was tied so that she could reach between her legs but couldn't untie her left hand. I watched as Emma faded and Eme appeared.

"You changed your mind," Eme said. "Come here." She held her hand out towards me.

I walked over and stopped just out of her reach. "I know how long you've been here. Emma doesn't know, but I do. I've seen you before. I didn't realize what I was seeing at the time, but now I understand." I backed up a step when she stretched to touch me. "No. That's not allowed."

"You want it," she said. "Look at what you did to me. You stripped me and tied me up. Let me do this to you. I promise you'll enjoy it." She tugged on the rope above her head.

"No. You don't have a say in what happens today. You will observe, and you will not interfere. The restraints are to protect Emma. I don't care what happens to you." I turned my back on her. "Let me talk to Emma."

Eme laughed. "No!"

"Maddie! Time for the backup plan!"

Maddie rushed in with a glass of wine in one hand and a syringe in the other. She stopped beside me and spoke to Eme. "You have a choice. You can drink the wine, or I can give you a shot of something to relax you. The doctor knows Emma well and was happy to help us."

Eme's eyes widened. "You put something in the wine. You drugged it."

"No," Maddie said. She took a sip and handed the glass to me. I took a sip. "It's just wine. Now this …" She shook the syringe. "I'm not sure what it is."

I held the wineglass and looked at Maddie. "Hold her arm still." I waited a moment to be sure Eme couldn't move her arm. Then I leaned over her and pressed the rim of the glass to her lips. "Drink it." I tipped the glass until the wine flowed into her mouth. Once she drank it all, I stepped away, pulling Maddie with me.

With a nod, Maddie left the room.

I waited.

"Do you really think that … will …" Eme stopped and stared at me. "Dawn. Eme's still here. She's fighting for control. I don't know how long I can last."

I lean over and kiss Emma tenderly on her lips. "Stay with me. Fight her. She wants me, not you. I will explain later, but now … Now you need to trust me."

"I do trust you."

I put my hand over hers and moved it between her legs. "I know you love all of us. Me. Maddie. Donna. Monna. But you neglect yourself. Every time you tried to take care of yourself, Eme appeared. You never realized it, but those times the days sped by too fast was because of Eme. She's controlling. I think she was created that very first day here when I appeared. I became a complete duplicate, but she stayed in your mind."

"She was jealous of your relationship with Dawn." Mother's voice sounded in the room. I hoped that meant she was stronger.

Emma didn't say anything, but I watched a tear roll down her cheek. "You need to love yourself. Mother will give you privacy now. Do you want me to help you or leave?"

"I don't know," Emma said.

"I have an idea," I whispered as I climbed on the bed next to her, pulling her into a hug. "Do what you need to do. I will hold you and keep you safe. Okay?"

She nodded.

I held her tight until I felt her body tense up and then shake a little, and then I held her a little longer. With a kiss to the top of her head, I asked, "Better?"

She nodded again. "Eme is gone. Mother came and took her after I ..." She looked up. "Please untie me."

"It's safe now," Mother said inside my head.

I untied the restraints and waited for Emma to dress. I felt my face warm at the thought of all that had happened in the last couple days. I turned to leave, but Emma's hand on my arm stopped me.

"Thank you, Dawn. I know you're embarrassed, but Eme manipulated you yesterday. I don't remember much of anything in the last few days. I don't know how long she was in control. I was lost, and you saved me." She opened the door and pulled Maddie into a hug. "I'm famished.

Didn't Eme ever eat?" She kissed each of us on the cheek, and I knew Emma was with us again.

Chapter 14

Sara and Em

Sara couldn't shake the feeling that she was being followed. Ever since leaving work, the same car had been behind her. It was a short drive home, and she rushed to get up the stairs to her apartment. She didn't waste time looking behind her. As she unlocked her door, she heard a man clear his throat. She turned and saw two men in dark suits wearing earpieces like she imagined the secret service probably wore.

"Are you Sara?" one of them asked. When she nodded, he said. "Em wants a meeting with you. We need to check the apartment first."

"Okay." It was the only word she could get out. They couldn't be serious. It must be a prank. Her friends knew Em was her favorite performer. She was even writing a book inspired by her music, but there was absolutely no way she could be there in her town in the middle of nowhere.

"It's okay. Send her up."

Sara dropped her lunch bag and purse on the table and waited. A moment later, Em stood inside her apartment. The men stepped outside and closed the door. Neither Em nor Sara said a word as they watched each other.

Sara was dressed in her work clothes. She wore beat up blue jeans, a pink t-shirt, white sneakers, and no makeup. In contrast, Em wore a black dress, fishnet stockings, high heels, and many rings and necklaces. Sara stared at her perfect, flawless makeup that only enhanced her blue eyes and blond hair.

"I've read your book."

Sara tried several times before her voice worked. "My book? How did you get my book? I only let one person see it."

"A friend of a friend of a friend of a friend." Em waved her hand. "I don't know how many friends were involved originally." She walked around, looking at everything in the small apartment.

"Originally? What? How long is the friends' chain now?" Sara watched her as she picked up random items and inspected them.

"Oh. I'm talking directly with your friend now. I've had her pass along my suggestions and feedback." She turned and looked Sara in the eye. "I've been enjoying your writing for several weeks."

Sara lost her balance and landed sideways on the edge of the couch before sliding to the floor. "Kari never said anything." Looking up, she saw Em holding out her hand. She ignored it and pushed against the couch to stand up. When she struggled to get to her feet, she felt a hand under her arm. "Thank you."

"I told Kari not to tell you." Em said. "I wanted to get to know you before I met you."

Sara walked past her and turned back. "Why?"

"You put your soul into your writing, and it's beautiful." She sat on the arm of the couch and watched Sara. "I have one question."

Sara paced as she waited for Em to ask her question. Her heart was pounding, and her mind was racing. When the question came, it was not at all what she expected. It stopped her instantly and left her standing in front of Em. She asked her to repeat herself because she didn't think she heard it right.

"Is your book a love letter to me?" Em asked.

They watched each other as Sara thought about it. After a long time, Sara answered. "Yes, but I never expected you to read it." The words tumbled from her lips, and her eyes opened wide at what she had revealed. As she moved to turn away, Em reached out with both hands. Losing her balance, she fell into Em's arms. "I never thought I would meet you." She gazed down into brilliant blue eyes as their lips met in a soft kiss.

Sara pulled away first. "This can't be real. You can't really be here. It's my mind playing tricks on me again." She backed away and walked in circles around the table until she collided with Em.

"Again?" Em held Sara's shoulders and looked into her eyes. "What happened?"

"They said the voice wasn't real. They locked me up for two weeks. They said it was for my own safety. They gave me drugs I didn't want. They said the voice would go away, and it did. It was horrible. I knew she was there, but my mind wouldn't let her in because of the drugs. When I passed all their tests, they let me go. It took days to get the drugs out of my system. Mother was so worried. She told me to write what she told me so I wouldn't forget." She grabbed Em's arms. "But you're here now. How? Did Mother send you to me? Is she the reason you read my writing?"

Em nodded as tears ran down her cheeks. "Yes."

With shaking hands, Sara reached up and wiped away Em's tears. "You fell in love with my writing."

"No," Em said. "Well, actually yes." She took Sara's hands in hers. "But I fell in love with you. I know you are more than your writing, but I saw your heart. I saw your soul. You are what I've been missing in my life. Mother knows that."

"So, you believe me? You believe Mother is real?" Sara asked.

"Yes. Emma, Dawn, Maddie, and all the others as well." She kissed Sara's hands. "Mother showed me when I read your book. How did you ...?"

"I've always loved your music. I know most people don't see it, but you show your heart when you perform. Then I kept seeing fan posted videos online. Most were from your shows, but some were taken when you were trying to live your life. I couldn't watch those. I yelled at the screen for them to leave you alone. I wanted to save you from them." Sara paused and squeezed Em's hands. "I watched your concerts and shows online. I know it's a performance and not real. You're acting along with the music, but with some songs the story feels too real. I wanted to jump through the screen and save you. I never want to see anyone treat you that way. I want to protect you. As I wrote about Emma, Dawn, Maddie, Monna, and Donna, I listened to you perform. I can't listen to the tracks on the albums. I want to hear live performances. I never realized I love you until today." She leaned forward until her head touched Em's. "How can we love each other when we only just met?"

Mother's voice sounded around them and in their heads. "Because you are soulmates."

* * *

Sara stretched and yawned before opening her eyes. Em was still asleep. Trying to avoid the squeaky spring in the bed, she rolled out of bed and stood. She heard the squeak a second before she was pulled back down. With a giggle she said, "I guess you weren't asleep."

"No, and where do you think you're going?" Em pulled her close for a kiss.

"I need coffee." Her face turned red. "And the bathroom. Do I have permission to go?"

Em kissed her again. "Breakfast too?"

"If you let me go."

Em nodded and released her. "You don't have to be embarrassed." She watched Sara hurry from the room and smiled. "You don't do this much, do you?"

"I never do this," Sara said. "It's been years since I've been with anyone, and I've never had anyone stay the night on the day we met."

Em walked into the kitchen behind Sara. "Do you regret last night?"

Sara spun around and kissed her. "Not at all."

They were interrupted by an insistent buzzing. Em rushed to grab her phone from the other room. After a short, muffled conversation, she returned. "I'm sorry. I need to go to a business meeting."

Sara grabbed her around the waist. "It's Saturday. Can't it wait?"

Em kissed Sara's cheek. "It won't take long. I will take you somewhere nice for lunch. I promise."

* * *

Sara jumped when her phone rang. It was loud, but she couldn't find it. Then she saw her lunch bag on the table and groaned. She never pulled her phone out to charge it Friday evening. She smiled when she remembered why. Then she hurried to grab the phone and plug it in.

"Of course, now it's gone to voicemail." She looked at the screen. "Work? What do they want on Saturday?"

When the notification popped up, she listened. "Sara, so sorry to bother you on a Saturday, but can you come in for about an hour? We are designing a new dress, and we're trying it on several people. We think one of the sizes will fit you. We would appreciate it if you could help out."

The message didn't ring true with Sara, and she ignored it. She had never helped with design. Her job was to run the machine that cuts the fabric. As she began dialing, she heard Mother's voice. "You need to go. They want to keep Em's secret. She has been working on a surprise for weeks."

Sara groaned. "She's designing a dress for me?"

"Yes, but I won't tell you more. You should go now. She's waiting for you."

She grabbed her phone and charger. "I only met her yesterday."

She felt Mother's warm presence all around. "That didn't matter when you lay in bed with her last night." She felt dizzy as she remembered. Mother laughed. "I didn't watch. Now go."

With a push from Mother's invisible hands, Sara grabbed her purse and headed out the door.

* * *

Sara put on the strange multi layered dress. It was the most horrible green she had ever seen, but she was assured the color was chosen simply because they had excess fabric. The dress was a test to see if the pattern worked well, but Sara suspected it was also a fitting for her. She didn't know what this could possibly be for.

"What are all these layers? It's heavy." She lifted the skirt a bit to see the layers of chiffon under the satin."

"It's versatile. Layers can be removed and added to give different looks. Now hold still while I check the fit." The young woman had a pincushion on her wrist and began pinning the dress to make it fit better. It took over an hour to pin all the layers into the best size and shape.

When they were done, Sara noticed Em watching her. "How long have you been here?"

"Long enough." There was a spark of mischief in her eyes. "Do you need help getting out of that?"

"Not from you," the young woman said. "I won't risk undoing my hard work."

"You can watch," Sara said, smiling.

* * *

Sara almost let her phone go to voicemail when Kari called. Before she could say anything, Kari blurted out, "Is she there? Did you meet her? What happened?"

"Kari? Did you accidentally drink coffee instead of tea today? You're never this hyper." Sara sat as she listened to her friend breathing hard. "Are you okay?"

"I'm okay, Sara. I'm just excited. Is Em there?"

"Yes. She was here when I got home from work yesterday." She glanced towards the bedroom. "Kari, she stayed here all night. Did you know?"

"What?" Kari asked. "What do you think I know?" She was silent for a moment. "Wait! She spent the night? What happened?"

"I am not telling you that!"

"I thought she was there to talk about the book."

Sara coughed. "We talked about the book for about five minutes."

"And then?" Kari asked.

"Let's say that I missed dinner and went straight to dessert."

"You naughty girl," Kari said.

"Kari, why did you share my writing?" She cleared her throat. "Did a voice in your head tell you to do it?"

"How did you know?"

"I need to tell you something, and please don't freak out." Sara waited until she heard a sound of agreement. "The story I wrote is real. Mother showed me everything. She talks to me."

After a short silence, Kari responded. Her voice was so quiet that Sara had trouble hearing her. "I've heard Mother too, but it wasn't her. She told me to call her Victoria, and she told me to share your story. When Em contacted me,

Mother told me it was safe to share with her. She wanted me to share it with her. Mother sent Em to us."

"Okay, but why did you keep it a secret?"

Kari didn't answer, but Mother did. Her voice filled Sara's head. "You weren't ready. I advised them to keep the secret."

"I'm sorry," Kari said.

"Do you know about the dress, too?" Sara asked.

"Dress? I don't know anything about a dress." Kari hummed a little. "Unless she's making the dresses in your book."

Sara scratched her forehead. "Why would she--? Oh my God!" She stood and paced as Kari repeatedly asked if she was okay. "I think I'm okay. Really. I've dreamed about this, but I can't get my hopes up. If I prepare myself for this, and I'm wrong, what happens?"

"Sara, stop and breathe. I can hear you pacing."

Sara stopped and took a deep breath. "I'm scared. It's great now, but what if it doesn't work out?"

Kari cleared her throat. "I don't care how famous she is. If she breaks your heart, I will personally come over there and teach her a lesson she will never forget. I told her that, too."

BROKEN PARALLELS

Chapter 15

The Festival

Sara fidgeted as people she'd never met styled her hair and applied makeup. Then they left her alone to change into new clothes. After several minutes, Em came into the bedroom to check on her.

"You haven't changed." Em pointed to the clothes laid out on the bed.

Sara stood staring at the bed, wearing only a bra, stockings, and panties. "I tried. I don't know how to put it on, and I didn't want them to help me." She felt her face get hot. "I don't want to cry and mess up my face, but I didn't know what to do." She caught a tear on her eyelashes before it could fall. "I'm sorry. I never wear makeup or clothes this fancy. Help me, please."

Em pulled her into an embrace. "I should have warned you, and I should have been here for you. I'm sorry."

As Em helped her into the soft pink dress, Sara smiled. "Where are we going? It's only dinner."

"Sorry we missed lunch." Em adjusted the skirt. "It's never just dinner when I go out. We need to look our best."

"But where are you taking me?" She grabbed the silver shoes, but Em stopped her.

"We forgot the underskirt," Em said.

Em held up a skirt made of chiffon in a rainbow of colors. Sara stepped into it and let Em lace it up in the back with a silver cord. When she dropped the dress back down over it, several inches of rainbow showed. It was so much like how she imagined Candra's wedding dress. She realized it was also like one of the layers of the dress from the fitting that morning.

"It will be beautiful when we dance." Em smiled and kissed her. "Now you can put on the shoes."

Sara stood still. "Where are we going?"

Em knelt down and slipped the shoes on Sara's feet over the silver fishnet stockings. "There's a festival downtown. I've been told several local restaurants will serve food."

"And there will be dancing?" Sara asked. "I'm not the best dancer."

Em kissed her knee before she stood. "Follow my lead, and you'll be fine."

"Is there something else happening tonight?" Sara took a few small steps to test the shoes.

"What else could possibly happen tonight?"

* * *

As Sara waited for security to check out the festival area, she looked around. She thought it was more of a big block party than a festival. There appeared to be one area that was sectioned off for dancing. Since they arrived, the music she heard was instrumental only. No one was singing. "I guess that makes it easier to talk to people."

"What?" Em asked.

"Sorry. I didn't realize I said that out loud. I just noticed all the music is instrumental only. It's nice."

The security team returned and stood outside the car. "People already know I'm here." Em held Sara's hand and kissed it. "You need to know what to expect."

"Okay." Sara felt her heart beat faster.

"Security will walk with us, but they won't crowd us. Try to ignore them. Their job is to stop any threats. We can interact with people, but if someone is suspicious, they will step in before they reach us. If you see someone you know, tell me. I can signal them. Understand?"

"Yes. Will people be taking photos?"

"Always. Videos too. It never ends." Em squeezed her hand. "If it's too much, we can leave."

After a moment, Sara shook her head. "No, I want to stay, but you must feed me. I'm starving."

After a brief kiss, Em knocked on the window. The door opened for them, and Sara was briefly blinded by flashing lights. Em pulled her close with a hand around her waist, and they both smiled and posed for the crowd. Sara thought they looked great together. Em wore black and gold with bright rainbow trim in strategic areas. It was a terrific contrast to the pink and silver with pastel rainbow trim that she wore. She swished her skirt and laughed as the crowd reacted to the brighter rainbow hidden in her skirt.

"This will be fun," she whispered to Em.

* * *

As the evening progressed, Sara wondered if the festival had been planned by Em. She never saw anything to indicate anyone else had organized it.

"Relax." It was Mother in her head again. "Don't overthink. She loves you and wants you to have fun. She chose food and music she knew you would enjoy."

After eating and dancing, Em found a microphone and asked for a pause of the music. The crowd groaned until she spoke to them. "Thank you all for coming to celebrate with us tonight. This is more than a Pride celebration. I have something special to share." She reached out her hand. "Sara, please join me." With a shaking hand, she took Em's and stood beside her on the small stage near the crowded dance floor.

"This is Sara. She is the love of my life." She lifted Sara's hand to her lips and kissed it. "And I have something I need to ask her tonight." She dropped to a knee in front of Sara. The crowd cheered. "Sara. You haven't known me very long, but I feel like we've known each other for a lifetime. I can't imagine my life without you." She released Sara's hand and took a jewelry box from someone nearby. She held out the box. "Will you marry me?"

The crowd was silent as they waited for an answer. Someone handed Sara a microphone. "The last twenty-four hours have been the best of my life because of you. Yes! I will marry you."

Em stood and pulled Sara close as the crowd went wild. Someone started the music again, but the crowd soon drowned it out. None of that mattered to them as they kissed. Neither knew when the microphones were taken from their hands. They were lost in each other, and the world, for a moment, ceased to exist.

Chapter 16

An Unexpected Complication

Sara squirmed in her seat during the car ride home. To distract herself, she asked the one question she'd never found an answer for. "Why is your professional name just the letter M? I know your name is Emma, and I call you Em. I always thought it should be spelled out with E and M."

Em squinted at her. "You had to ask that. It's not that interesting. It was a mistake. In an interview before I was famous, I was asked my name. The reporter didn't hear it all. He thought I said Em, but when the story was printed, it had a typo of just the letter M. Even though they printed a correction later, it stuck. Everyone used it when they wrote about me. I suppose it contributed to my success in the beginning."

Sara yawned and laid her head on Em's shoulder. "But Emma is short for another name, isn't it?"

"Yes, but I suspect you know that name already." Em patted Sara's leg. "You've been awake too long. Let's go back to my hotel. It's closer than your apartment." She saw the driver nod that he heard.

* * *

Sara opened her eyes when she heard knocking and realized she wasn't in her apartment. Em was talking with someone at the door. "What's going on?" Sara asked.

Em turned and smiled as a man pushed a cart into the room. Em handed him a tip before closing the door behind him. "I ordered breakfast."

Sara went straight for the coffee before sitting at the small table. "I enjoyed myself last night."

"It was enjoyable, but we need to talk."

Sara nearly spit out her coffee. "Was it all a publicity stunt? Are you going to take the ring back?"

Em knelt down in front of Sara and took her face in both hands. "No. No. I'm sorry. I shouldn't have said it that way. I love you and want to marry you." She kissed her. "We need to talk about social media." She stood and grabbed the plates of food. "Eat while we talk."

"Is social media a problem?"

Em sat across the table from her. "It can be. I want you to stay offline for a while. Avoid television and radio too. I know you have friends. You can send them a message that you need to detox from social media." She took a bite from her plate as she waited for a reaction.

"Can I still call and text my close friends?"

146

"You can keep in contact with your friends, but they can't send you news stories." Em reached across the table and caressed Sara's hand.

"Okay. I'm sure Kari is going crazy because we haven't talked since before the festival." Sara looked around. "Where is my phone?"

"You're not upset?" Em asked.

"I've seen what reporters and fans do to you. Do you think that will happen to me?" She continued looking around the room.

"My assistant has your phone. She's checking all your social media and muting accounts that could be a problem. Notifications will be turned off for most things. I hope you will be spared the worst of it, but you are new in my life. That attracts all types." Em turned at the sound of the door opening. "Gina, is there a problem?"

"Not at all, Em. I'm done with the phone, but Kari has called many times. She's on the phone now. I'll put it on speaker." She tapped the screen and set the phone on the table.

"Sara! You're engaged! Are you excited?"

"Hello, Kari," Em said. "Before I let you talk, there are rules now. Please don't tell us anything that was said about last night. No news reports or social media. Understand?"

"Yes. Gina explained it to me."

"Good," Em said as Gina nodded.

"Hi, Kari," Sara said. "It was amazing. I'm still exhausted from all of it and trying to drink my coffee."

Kari laughed. "How can you be so calm? I was a nervous wreck for a week after Em talked to me the first time, but you're engaged after less than two days. This is crazy!"

"Calm down, Kari. Drink some tea."

Gina cleared her throat. "There is something from last night that both Kari and I noticed. You need to know."

"What?" Em and Sara asked together.

Kari coughed. "Sorry. Choked on my tea. At the same time you went live, someone claiming to be Em went live and announced a new song release coming at the end of the month. She looked so much like you, Em, but her hair was much darker. It looked like she wore colored contacts because her eyes looked black and red. It felt wrong."

"I'll take it from here, Kari. Thanks," Gina said. "Your live stream had twenty times the views, but people are sharing hers. There's a possibility that someone used artificial intelligence to simulate you making an announcement, but I doubt it. It doesn't have the usual flaws seen in A.I. generated videos."

Sara shivered. "It's Eme. The one who tried to hurt Dawn and Emma. I can feel it. I dreamed about her last night, but maybe it wasn't a dream."

Em turned to Gina. "Thank you. You can go now. I know I don't need to remind you to keep this confidential. Don't tell anyone."

Gina put her fingers to her lips and turned them as if locking them with a key. "Promise," she said before leaving.

"Kari, can you keep an eye on this for us?"

"I will do anything to keep the two of you safe."

"Thank you," Sara said.

"This is going to be messy. We should get married before she releases her song."

"Really?" Kari asked from the phone.

"Yes," Sara and Em said as one.

Chapter 17

Unexpected Visitors

Sara twirled around and smiled as Em's team took photos and videos to be shared later. The pastel rainbow lifted to reveal a bright rainbow every time she spun around. She posed and danced in all the many combinations possible with the dress.

She stumbled as she finished the photoshoot. Then she heard her phone ring. Still in the dress, she answered. "Kari, is there a problem? I can feel something isn't right."

"Eme released the song early. It's out now. A repulsive man contributed to the song. It's going crazy online. It's all hateful lyrics. I feel dirty after hearing it. Could it be Harvey?"

Sara leaned against the wall to keep from falling over. "Oh God. I hope not. How are they here? I thought Mother took care of them. Thanks, Kari. I need to go find Em."

"I've got your back, Sara."

"I know." Sara hung up and got changed as quickly as possible, making apologies to everyone before leaving with her security team.

Her calls to Em kept going straight to voicemail as she tried to call on the drive to the hotel. "She'd better be on the phone with people who can help us."

"She is, but it won't be enough." The female voice was in her head, but it wasn't Mother.

"Who are you?" She asked, hoping security would think she was talking on her phone with her earbuds. She didn't need them thinking she was crazy.

"I'm Victoria. Nathan is here, too. We have talked to Kari." After a moment, she continued. "Mother is Em's mother. We are your ancestors from a long time ago. We've come to help."

"Help? How?" Sara turned her phone to silent so she wouldn't be interrupted.

"Eme and Harvey are here to spread hate. It's spreading slowly now, but it will gain traction if it's not stopped soon. Mother may have a plan, but it's a temporary fix. You have ancient magic that can stop it permanently," Victoria said.

"We don't have time to explain in detail." The new voice was male. She guessed it was Nathan. "Only you can protect people from his poison. Em has magic too. Donna, Emma, Monna, Maddie, and Dawn have it too, but it's strongest in Em. They will spread love to combat the hate, but you need to do your part."

* * *

Sara heard Em arguing with herself as she approached the hotel room, but what she saw inside the room was not what it sounded like at all. Every good version of Em was in the room as well as Candra and Cassie. They were exactly like she saw them in her mind. When Em saw her, she swept her up into her arms and kissed her. "Mother brought them."

Sara looked around the room and nodded to each of them. "Dawn. Emma. Cassie. Donna. Maddie. Monna. Candra. I'm Sara. Have you heard from Victoria and Nathan or just Mother?"

"Victoria spoke to them." The voice came from Maddie, but it was Mother speaking. Sara knew it from her dreams.

"What is your plan?" Sara asked.

"We were discussing that," Emma said. "The new song will climb the charts. It's becoming more popular every day. We can't stop it."

"Of course, you can," Sara said. "You need to knock it down with better songs."

"We don't have that many new songs," Em said.

"But you have at least one new song. I know you've been writing one for the wedding. You just need to remix enough old songs."

"There's no time for that," Dawn said.

A male voice sounded in the room. "You need a live performance. Remix as you perform. Record as you go. The magic works best if it's a live song."

Maddie spoke in Mother's voice. "Don't wait to book a venue. Em can go downtown and convince people to close off the block like they did for the engagement party. Go tonight and set it up for tomorrow. All of us will go and take turns performing. It will go all day. People will stream it everywhere."

"You must call out the imposter before the concert begins," Nathan said. "Em, it must be you. Mother, Victoria, and I will be with you to strengthen the magic."

"Cassie and Candra should watch online traffic," Victoria said. "I suspect there will be live totals of listeners."

"But now, there is something even more important we need to do right now," Mother said. "Sara and Em need to be married right away. You have the license. Gina already signed the marriage certificate for us. I will perform the ceremony. Everyone ready?"

"Do we have a choice?" Em asked.

"I don't think so," Sara said.

The ceremony was more of a handfasting than a wedding. Mother in Maddie's body spoke in a language they didn't understand as she wove silver and gold ribbons around their clasped hands. They glowed brighter with every word until the room was bathed in a warm glow. When they kissed, everyone felt it. When the glow faded, the ribbons were gone; instead, there were faint marks on both their arms and hands where the ribbons had been a moment before.

Victoria joined Mother in Maddie, and they moved from person to person around the room. Each of them glowed for several seconds before they moved to the next person.

Sara felt Nathan join Mother and Victoria when they reached her. They spoke with one voice inside her head. "You will distract the imposter when she finds you tomorrow. Keep her from listening or watching any live performances. She will try to make you believe she is your Em. Remember, what she really wants is you. You are her weakness. Tomorrow evening, you will join the others on stage where your magic will strengthen theirs. Do you understand?"

"I understand."

Chapter 18

A Magical Performance

Sara wanted to arrive at her job early. She needed to give her boss a heads up about Eme, but Eme knocked on her apartment door before she left home. "Em, did you lose your key?" Eme squeezed past her into the apartment, spanking her along the way. Her hair was dark and straight; her eyes were dark. Sara did her best to smile at her. "I'm on my way to work. You can come with me. My boss won't mind."

Eme spun around and grabbed her. Her grip was too tight as she kissed Sara with too much tongue. "Okay, but I might want a quickie in the bathroom later."

Sara took a few slow breaths and said, "Sure. Whatever you want."

Eme kept her hand on Sara's leg for the entire drive to work. Sara ignored it. Eme turned on the radio. It was too early to hear the live stream, but that new song was playing.

It was impossible to tell what the words were. Too many were censored. "You need a satellite radio. Then we could listen to it all."

Once inside at work, Sara slipped a note to her boss. She hoped it explained that this Eme was an imposter. She wore an earbud in her ear that connected to a spare phone in her lunch bag. She could listen and know when the live stream started.

It wasn't bad. Eme got bored and tried to grope her a few times. After the live stream had been going on for a few hours, Sara heard the new song, the one that should have been for the wedding. Eme grabbed her hard, trying to pull her to the bathroom. Sara shoved her against the wall. "Look. I know exactly who you are. You are not my Em. You will never be as good as her. I won't call you by her name. I won't call you that name from your song either. You want that, and you will never get satisfaction from me. No one here is listening to your song. We're listening to real music."

In her head, Sara heard Mother tell her they had done enough but would keep the concert going for much longer. The fans wanted it.

"No one wants your song anymore," Sara said. "You're being knocked down. When the charts are updated next week, your song won't be on it."

"That's impossible. You're bluffing." Eme pushed away from her and grabbed her phone. She opened app after app on her phone. "What is this? No one can release that many songs in one day. Where is she?"

"I'm not going to tell you. You can't have her." Sara stared into her dark eyes. "You can't have me either. We got married yesterday, and Mother bound it with magic. You can't break it."

Sara saw her boss standing behind Eme. He mouthed, "Are you okay?" She shook her head slightly. He mouthed, "Can I help?" She nodded slightly. Out loud he said, "I have someone coming in to perform maintenance on your machine. Maybe you should call it a day."

"Okay. It felt like the machine wasn't working well anyway." Sara grabbed her things and walked out. She felt Eme following her. Once outside, she shoved her things in her car and locked it. She pulled her phone from her pocket and pulled up the video of the very start of the live stream. She held it up for Eme to see and hear.

Em was on stage speaking. "Thank you for joining me today. I hope you enjoy the music. If you have requests, I will try to do as many as I can. I'll be here all day." She seemed to glow as she continued. "Before I begin, I need to address a serious situation. People often sing my songs and remix my songs. I'm always flattered. It means they enjoy my music. That's why I make music. However, there is an imposter out there right now pretending to be me, and she released a song under my name. It's a hateful song that I can't endorse. It spreads hate like a disease. That's why I'm spreading love today. Everyone has my permission to film and share every song I perform today as long as you keep my name on it. Spread the love. Keep it going. To the imposter, I know who you really are. I know where you are. This ends today."

Eme grabbed the phone from Sara's hand and threw it across the parking lot. "Where is she?"

"I will never tell you," Sara said before she vanished.

* * *

Sara appeared backstage in the middle of all the Em look-a-likes. They were working hard to look and act the same, and for the first time, she couldn't tell them apart. Then Em kissed her. "Are you okay?" Em asked.

Sara nodded. "But I will need a new phone. She smashed mine."

"Did you hear the new song?" Em asked.

"Part of it. She interrupted it. Will you sing it again?"

"I would love to sing it again." She took Sara's hand. "We're going on stage when Emma finishes her songs. It's been easy to keep going so long with each of us performing. Dawn even sang a few." Em pushed hair back from Sara's ear and pulled out the earbud she'd forgotten was there. She held up a different device. "You need this earpiece. On stage, you can't hear yourself. It's too loud. This will let you hear the band, my microphone, your microphone, and sometimes the audience when it's needed." She helped get the earpiece in place. "Does that feel secure?"

Sara nodded. "I'm ready. I might throw up from the butterflies in my stomach, but I'm ready."

Someone handed her a skirt. "It's Maddie, and you need a quick costume change," she said. "Your top looks great, but slip on this skirt."

Sara pulled on the long pink skirt and slipped her pants off after. Maddie grabbed the pants and pulled off her shoes. She slipped Sara's feet into silver sandals. "Thanks, Maddie."

When Emma came backstage, she hugged Sara. "The crowd just requested your song."

Em led Sara onto the stage, and the crowd roared. "This is Sara. We have some news. Yesterday, we were married. This is the song I wrote for her."

I saw you in words, a gift from your muse.
You knew all my thoughts and fears,
The real me, not the image for the news.

Share my light. Share my soul.
Look into my eyes. Never let me go.

My soul laid bare for you, I never knew
You prayed for me night and day
To keep me safe from those that prey.

Share my light. Share my soul.
Look into my eyes. Never let me go

Your heart. Your soul. I saw them both.
In your eyes, I lost myself.
You'll never be by yourself.

Share my light. Share my soul.
Look into my eyes. Never let me go

Hold me now. Never let me go.
Let the magic keep us together,
Now and into forever.

Share my light. Share my soul.
Look into my eyes. Never let me go
Never let me go. Never let me go.

After the song, Em and Sara shared a kiss to the cheering of the crowd. "Now," Em said. "I've heard Sara sing. She's really good. Maybe if you request something simple, she'll sing it with me."

Sara felt a warmth growing inside her. When Em took her hand, it intensified. By the gasp from the crowd, she knew they were glowing. She didn't remember hearing the song request, and she barely remembered singing. She did remember that all the others backstage joined them, and she thought she heard Mother and Victoria too. They sang three songs. By the end, the crowd was singing along. In her ear, she heard Candra talking about the internet reaction. In fans' live streams, crowds of people watching everywhere were singing along. People stopped whatever they were doing to listen and sing along. Sara and Em smiled at each other as the song ended. The music echoed all around for several seconds. Then Em kissed Sara, and the crowd cheered.

Chapter 19

Concert Interrupted

Sara watched the concert from backstage as it continued into its eleventh hour. She had watched for hours, and Em pulled her onstage to perform with her every time she went. It was all going well until they heard Dawn scream.

The sun was setting as Dawn played an instrumental version of a fan favorite on guitar. Out of the shadows, Harvey and Eme climbed onto the stage and grabbed her. The guitar fell as Dawn screamed.

Sara rushed to the stage before Em could stop her. She knew the others wouldn't follow her because the illusion of one true Em would be broken, but Cassie followed her.

"She's not who you want," Sara said. She wore a microphone hooked around her ear. The whole world could hear her. "I'm here. I know you searched and couldn't find me. You got my attention with that song. I know who you really are, Regina. I know you, too, Harvey."

Eme took the microphone from Dawn's hand. "And we know who all of you are. Would you like me to tell the people of this world about Emma, Monna, Maddie, Donna, and Dawn?" She ran the back of her hand down Dawn's cheek.

Out of the corner of her eye, Sara saw Cassie creep forward. She shook her head a little, and Cassie stopped. "Regina, do you think anyone would care?"

"Stop calling me that! I'm Em!" She released Dawn and walked towards Sara.

"It doesn't matter what name you use," Sara said. "It won't change who you are."

Emma walked past Sara and stopped in front of Eme. "Are you one of us?" She turned and waved her hand to the others walking onto the stage. The crowd broke their silence, and Sara could hear ripples of conversation all around. Emma reached out to touch Eme, but Eme flinched back.

"Don't touch me!"

Emma stood taller. When she spoke again, her voice had changed. "I recognize your soul. I remember that you don't like to be touched. You want to be the one in control." Emma turned a glare on Harvey. "I suggest you release her." When he tightened his grip on Dawn's arm, Emma raised her hand. He released Dawn and flew across the stage.

Inside Sara's head, Victoria said, "Mother's angry."

"I know you Eme." Emma turned back to Eme as Mother spoke. "I know you Eme. You ran from me and found this woman named Regina who resembles my daughters." She paused and tilted her head as she looked at

Eme. "No. Somehow, she is one of my daughters. I assume she came here when my husband accidentally opened a rift between my worlds." She shook her head. "I will deal with that later. Now I want to address the problem you created. You took over Regina's body, but you couldn't completely control her. She changed her hair and eyes. I can feel her fighting you. Let her go and come home."

"No. I like it here."

Sara walked over to stand next to Emma. "But why do you want me?"

Something in Eme's expression changed. Before Sara had time to react, she felt a hand on her shoulder as Eme reached out and grabbed her hand. Then the world went black.

*　*　*

Inside Sara's head, Mother argued with Nathan and Victoria. She couldn't understand the words, but she knew they were confused and angry. She couldn't see or feel anything. "Where am I?" Her voice sounded wrong. "What happened?" She thought her voice sounded dead. "Someone talk to me!"

"Sara," Mother said. "Harvey's touch sent you to us. We're trying to send you back."

"Back where?" Sara asked.

"To the world of the living," Victoria said.

"I'm dead?"

"Not if I have a say in it," Mother said.

"I told you," Nathan said. "We need help from out there. We must hope Regina still has some good in her. If Harvey destroyed it all, you may not find your way back."

"We need to find them," Mother said.

"My Em," Sara said. "Does she know?"

"Show her," Victoria said.

"Time moves differently here," Nathan said. "While we've talked, only seconds have passed there. I can show you your Em and those with her. However, Harvey has blocked me from showing you yourself, Eme, and him. I don't know how he's doing it."

"Please," Sara said. "Let me see my wife."

The darkness gave way to a foggy image of the stage. Em reached out to where Sara had been a few seconds earlier. She stood still for a few seconds before her eyes went wide. Falling to her knees, she screamed, "Sara! No!" Everyone dropped to help her as the crowd fell silent again. "She's gone. Harvey killed her." She fell into Emma's arms and sobbed. "No!"

One voice in the crowd began to sing. It was quiet, but as others joined it grew louder. It wasn't recognizable at first, but once everyone in the crowd was singing together, Em recognized the wedding song. It was hauntingly beautiful being sung a'cappella by so many people. She cried harder.

After several minutes, she found her voice. "Thank you." She choked on the words. "I know it must be strange to learn about magic this way. Thank you for staying here with me after seeing the truth." She felt a warmth throughout her body as she heard a murmur from the crowd. "Mother?"

"Yes." Mother's voice filled the air. "I need to speak with my daughters privately. You are all beautiful. Keep the music going. It lifts their spirits."

Sara listened as Mother spoke to her children in a voice only they could hear. "Sara is not lost to us. Victoria and Nathan are with her. We have tried to find Regina, Harvey, and Sara's body with no luck."

Em cried out, and Dawn hugged her even as Emma squeezed her tighter.

Mother continued, "Harvey is blocking us, but there's still a chance. If Regina and Eme work together, they can bring her back. Harvey's touch caused this. I think he wants to bring her back, but his magic is incompatible with Sara's. If any of you were to find them, you might be able to bring her back, but you would risk being touched by Harvey. I don't want to lose any more children."

* * *

Sara watched Em as she cried. "If I don't return to her, she will find me. How long until I can't go back?"

"As long as one of us is here with you," Victoria said, "forever."

"But we want you back with Em where you belong," Nathan said. "We can make the time pass more quickly for you here. Waiting hours while only minutes pass there is torture, but it was necessary when you first arrived."

Sara didn't know how much time passed as she talked with Victoria and Nathan about music, magic, and love. They are all intertwined. "Is Mother's magic different from yours and mine," Sara asked. "And where does Harvey's magic come from?"

"Your magic and ours is from centuries ago. It's passed down through generations by blood," Nathan said. "It's been weak for several generations. Your magic is stronger, and we strengthened it even more. We think Harvey has old magic as well, but it's not the same as ours. While we can strengthen magic already present in someone, he seems to be able to gift it to people. He did that in the world Mother destroyed. We don't fully understand his magic."

"And Mother?" Sara asked.

"We don't know where she got her magic," Victoria said. "She doesn't know either. All she knows is that when she inhabits a body, they have a bit of magical ability when she leaves them. It's stronger in some than others."

"Where am I?"

The voice sounded like Eme.

Chapter 20

Stuck Between Worlds

"I'm not sure where we are, but I think we're supposed to be dead," Sara said. "I refuse to remain dead."

"Sara? I'm so sorry. Harvey was controlling me," Eme said. "He didn't have a use for me anymore. He said he was going to kill me. I guess he did. Is Regina here too?"

"I don't know if she's alive or not," Victoria said. "She didn't pass through here."

"How do we get back?" Eme asked.

"I don't know," Sara said. "You were supposed to be my way back. "Victoria, can you show us what's happening back there? Is Mother helping everyone?"

As the image of the world returned, Nathan said, "She is comforting the grieving."

"How much time has passed? Sara asked.

"Two days," Victoria said.

"Two days," Sara said as she watched Em. "She must feel like she's dying."

* * *

Em curled up on Sara's bed as she cried. Mother's touch glowed all around. "Has anyone found them?" Em asked.

Emma lay next to her and pulled her close. "No, but we'll find her."

"This is dangerous," Mother said. "Harvey will be waiting."

Em grabbed a tissue and blew her nose. "I don't care. He took my wife from me. I want to find him and make him pay."

Emma smoothed back her hair and kissed her forehead. "Maybe together we will be strong enough to fight him."

"Strength isn't going to stop him," Mother said.

"We need to do something!" Em threw the box of tissues against the wall.

Dawn looked in from the hallway. "We have a possible sighting. One of the fan groups near here thinks they saw Harvey. It doesn't mean Sara is close. As we know, he can teleport himself anywhere."

Em jumped out of bed and changed into fresh clothes. "Let's go."

Dawn blocked the doorway. "We should call the police and let them check it out. It's in a high crime area."

Em pushed her out of the way. "I don't care. I have to find her."

"Mother, can't you look and see if she's there?" Emma asked.

"No. Harvey has blocked me from seeing where he's been. I don't know how he does it."

Em grabbed her keys. "Why didn't you tell me this earlier? We can go to the place you can't see."

"No," Mother said. "He planned this well in advance. He blocked places all over the world. They could be anywhere. He planned to take Sara, but I don't think he intended to kill her. That was an accident. Nathan thinks his touch killed her because their magics clashed. I think he wants her to come back, but his touch keeps it from happening."

"It's been forty-eight hours," Emma said. "Why do you think she can still be brought back to us?"

"Because I can't live without her," Em said. She snatched a piece of paper from Dawn. "Are you coming? I'm going with or without you."

Em ignored her security team and drove to the address on the paper. Emma and Dawn rode with her. Several times along the way, they saw fights breaking out on the street. As they passed, the fighting stopped, and the people stared at them. Many people wearing hats removed them and held them over their hearts.

"It's like being in a funeral procession," Emma whispered. "They know, and they're showing respect."

Dawn looked out the back window. "And they're following us. Do you think it's the magic?"

Emma turned and watched the growing crowd behind them. "I don't think they're here to hurt us."

Em stopped the car. "I don't think he's here." A tap on the window made her flinch. She rolled down the window when she saw the girl with blue hair dressed in black.

"He was here, Em." She leaned against the car as she talked. "We ain't never seen them girls. We searched inside for you, but we got your back if you wanna check." She bent and looked into the car at Dawn and Emma. "Wow! It's true. You all look the same." She backed up as Em opened the door. "I promise we won't hurt you. We're here to help."

Em got out and hugged the girl. "Thank you. What's your name?"

"I'm Christa." She waved her hand at the crowd. "These are my girls in the front. I don't know about all them back there. How'd the fighting stop when you rolled through?"

"Magic."

Inside the vacant building, Em wandered around with Dawn and Emma until they found what Dawn called a nest. "He's been here," Em said.

"Look." Dawn angled her phone so the flashlight illuminated the wall. They saw a message written in large red letters. "I hope that's not blood."

Em clutched her heart as she read it. "You're seven steps behind. Learn the pattern. Maybe you'll find me."

Emma touched the wall. "I think it's paint."

* * *

Sara watched from too far away. "What is he doing? Why is he leading them on?"

After a long silence, Eme answered. "Before we took you, we went to many places. I don't know where we were, but in each place, he left a message like this. He started with seven steps behind and ended with eighty steps ahead. Only one indicated the right place. I wish I knew where. I would tell you. I don't know what the numbers mean."

"But why?" Sara asked.

"I think he wants Em to see him as he uses you to rule the world."

After watching Em visit more places Harvey had been, Sara screamed. In this dark dead place, it wasn't satisfying. She didn't think she actually had a voice. All she thought she heard was her projected thoughts. It was all consciousness, no body. "Nathan, Victoria, I know I can't go back to my body until someone revives me, but can I go back into another body?"

"I wouldn't advise it," Nathan said.

"Mother does it. You did it. Why can't I?" Sara asked.

"I didn't say you can't. I said I wouldn't advise it. It's risky. Mother and I have had practice. Where would you go?"

"It's obvious," Victoria said. "She wants to guide Em. We should help her. If she's anything like others in our family, she will do it with or without our help. It's best to support her."

"Alright," Nathan said. "Stay here with Eme. I will help Sara."

* * *

Emma and Maddie watched Em as she paced. She was wearing Sara's clothes and wore her hair like Sara. "I have to find her. I won't accept that she's gone." When she turned, she stumbled and fell to her knees. "Sara?"

Monna rushed to help her. "Sara's not here. We haven't found her."

"She's in my head." Em stood up with their help. "She wants to talk to you and Emma."

Em's voice changed as Sara spoke through her. "It's me. I don't know how long I can stay. I need to see Em's upcoming tour schedule. I think it has the answer." She walked to the wall where photos of each of Harvey's messages were pinned.

Emma brought a tablet showing the tour dates. "Do you think the steps away are referring to show dates?"

"Yes, but do we count only show dates or all days on the calendar? Do we count the special appearances at festivals too?" Sara said.

"Each of us try one possibility." Candra grabbed pens and some paper. "Only one should work with all his messages."

"Does Harvey know about the festivals?" Emma asked.

"We should assume he knows everything." Sara started writing. "I will look at all the tour dates and festivals. Emma, you look at just the tour. Maddie, can you look at calendar dates?"

Emma and Monna both nodded as they huddled over the tablet on the table.

An hour later, Em threw her pen across the room. "Sorry. That was me. Em. Sara and I are frustrated. We must be missing something. None of these work with or without the festival appearances."

"Add in the wedding date. The date you originally planned for it." Dawn picked up the pen from the floor and joined them at the table. "He's angry about the wedding." She started making corrections to each of the lists. "I wish I knew why he touched me without hurting me, but his touch killed Sara. If we knew that, we could use it against him. Mother is afraid, but I don't think we're in as much danger as she thinks." She opened a map on the tablet. "Miami. That's what the numbers say, but I don't think Sara's in Miami." She tapped a spot off the coast of Florida. "I think she's on our island."

Emma gasped. "He's trying to use the pocket universe. He doesn't want to rule this world. He wants to rule all of them."

Em paced as she mumbled to herself for a while. "I don't understand. Sara is trying to explain. I read her book about you and these universes, but I really don't know how Harvey can rule over them all."

"Book? About us?" Maddie asked.

Dawn shushed her. "Not important right now."

Mother's voice sounded throughout the apartment. "He wants to be God."

Chapter 21

Back to the Island

Everyone talked at once, Sara couldn't understand anything. Then Mother silenced them with her words. "I will die again before I let him become a god." She glowed around Em as she spoke to Sara. "You need to recharge. Let Nathan take you back to the safe place between worlds. He and Victoria will give you strength. You will be back with us soon." She glowed brighter, enveloping everyone in the room. "I need to visit our island. John needs to start an evacuation."

Maddie stifled a cry. "John. He's with the children."

"I will keep them safe," Mother said. "I promise."

"It's a trap," Sara said as she felt Nathan pulling her away. When they were back with Victoria and Eme, she tried to go back on her own, but she was stuck. "We have to do something. How do I go back? Mother can't face him alone. I don't understand how he planned this."

"You can't go back yet, and I don't know how he planned it. He's been mostly invisible to us," Nathan said.

175

"He knew that song I sang would cause trouble," Eme said. "He counted on you and Em to do something big to stop it. He doesn't care about the music. It was just a tool."

"He waited until we were vulnerable," Sara said.

"He's going to trap Mother and use her to open portals to as many worlds as he can," Victoria said. "We can't allow that. We must help."

"First we need to find volunteers to let us borrow their bodies," Nathan said.

"What about Christa and her friends?" Sara asked.

"The girl gang?" Eme asked.

"I think they would be perfect if they agree," Victoria said. "They are strong women."

"We need them to be strong," Nathan said. "It won't only be the four of us. We need as many of your ancestors as we can gather. We will need all their magic. Victoria, see how many you can find while I teach Sara how to use her magic. Sara, you will need it when you return to your body."

"We don't have time for all this," Sara said. She felt a warm touch from Nathan.

"You forget that time means nothing here. While it always moves forward, I can slow it enough to virtually stop it temporarily," Nathan said. "First, your magic is tied to your soul rather than your body. What I teach you will work in Christa's body or yours."

"Victoria and I talked," Eme said. "She thinks Mother is wrong. Mother said strength won't defeat Harvey, but we think strength is the key. His magic is different, and it's strong. If your magic is stronger, you might have a chance."

"A chance," Sara said. "I hope it's more than a chance."

"May I continue?" Nathan asked. "Or would you rather debate than take action?" When Sara and Eme remained silent, he asked, "Do you want a few smaller lessons, or do you want everything at once?"

"I don't know," Sara said. "Do whichever makes the most sense to you."

"All at once then so you can better see the relationships between the magics. It may be disorienting. I'm sorry."

Sara felt Nathan's presence more intimately as images, thoughts, and feelings flooded through her. When Nathan finished and left her alone, she sensed others around her. Hundreds of souls were ready to help.

"Okay," Sara said. "Let's go find Christa."

* * *

Sara watched as Christa looked all around, trying to find the voice or a camera. She couldn't blame the girl. The first time she heard Mother, she thought someone was playing a joke on her. After several minutes of Nathan and Victoria trying to talk to her, Sara interrupted. "Christa, I'm Sara. I need your help to find my body so I can return to Em. It will be dangerous, but it will help Em."

At the mention of Em, Christa froze. "She alright? She sure was angry when you wasn't here."

"She's okay, but she needs help. I need help. You and your girls are strong. We need that. You will still be there, but we will be in control. I promise we won't hurt you, and you might have some magic when it's all over."

"Magic?" Christa looked at her girls. "Could be fun." She looked around, trying to see Sara. "Where you at?"

"If you say yes, I'll be in your head," Sara said. "If you're strong enough, others will join us. We will make you even stronger."

"Girls?" They all nodded. "Yes."

The group glowed as Sara as her family merged with them. "I need to see Em and the others. Can we keep an eye on them as we go?"

"We can stop and get them," Nathan said.

"No," Sara said. "She needs motivation from my absence, but I need to know what they're doing. If they don't have a way to get to the island, we need to provide one."

* * *

Donna held Em as she cried. "Don't leave us, Em. We can find her and bring her back. We know where she is now."

Em looked up at everyone from where she sat on the floor. "Sara left. Mother left. Nathan left. How do we get there in time?"

"Do you have a van or limo?" Maddie knelt down next to them. "If we all get into one car, Mother's husband can get us there. That's the only way."

"Mother said you would need me." The male voice echoed all around them. "Hurry. We don't want Mother angry at us."

Em sniffed. "Is that him?"

"Oh dear. You're a new one. Come on. We can't delay. There's a car outside."

* * *

Christa/Sara smiled when she saw Em at the island bridge, but Em was still crying when they hugged. "I'm so glad to see you made it here." Before she could kiss her, Em pushed her away.

"Christa, why are you here?" Em held her at arm's length. "You shouldn't have come."

"Em, it's me." Christa/Sara moved Em's arm and grabbed her face in both hands. "I borrowed Christa to get here."

In her head, Christa said, "Kiss her. That will convince her."

Christa/Sara leaned forward and kissed Em, letting all her pent-up emotions flow through her. Em was stiff and unresponsive at first, but she relaxed and pulled Sara into a tight embrace. The air around them crackled. When they separated, Christa/Sara wiped tears from Em's eyes. "I love you."

"I love you too."

"We brought reinforcements." Christa/Sara pointed to the other girls. "Nathan, Victoria, and please don't overreact, but Eme is here too. She's rid of Harvey's influence now." She stared Em in the eyes to make sure she understood. When Em nodded, she continued. "My family has a history of magic that goes back centuries. My ancestors have come to help. Each of us has hundreds of them with us, contributing magic to fight Harvey." She looked around. "Have you found Harvey and my body yet?"

Em shook her head. "We arrived right before you did. I don't feel Mother. Do you think she's in the other world?"

"I hope not. It's a trap."

A girl with blue and white striped hair stepped up on a rock. She was tall, but now she stood taller than everyone. She spoke with such confidence and authority, that everyone knew it was Nathan speaking through her. "We must split up and search. One of us with each group. Victoria will go with Cassie and Donna. I will go with Monna and Candra. Sara and Em will stay together. Emma, are you okay to take Eme with Dawn and Maddie? If you have trouble, call for Nikki to help with the magic. We didn't teach Eme the magic, but it should be instinctual."

Emma nodded. "We understand her. She can come with us."

Maddie passed around radios to each group. "I didn't know if our phones would work. If you find something, let everyone know."

"Em and I will take the trail that leads to the diner in the other world. It goes straight to the center of town." Christa/Sara took Em's hand and started walking as the other groups picked their paths.

"How do you know the way?" Em ducked under a low tree branch.

"I saw this place when I was writing. Remember? Also, I feel something pulling me in this direction. Maybe I'm drawn to my body, but I'm hoping it's Mother. We need her strength." Sara stepped over a fallen tree.

Em paused before stepping over the tree. "Are you sure this is the correct path?"

Christa/Sara held out her free hand for a moment and the trail glowed. "That's how I see it."

Em stopped and peered down the trail. It shone bright even in the daylight. "How did you do that? Have you always been able to do magic?"

Christa/Sara laughed. "I've always had the ability, but I didn't know it. Nathan showed me how to use it earlier today."

They resumed walking down the path, stepping over logs when they blocked the way. A few times, they climbed over large rocks. "This can't be the right way." Em untangled her hair from a low tree branch. "We're lost, aren't we?"

"Do you think Harvey would make it easy for you?" The question came from Christa, but the voice wasn't Sara's or Christa's.

Em turned and looked at her. "I suppose not." She looked back at the trail. "What's your name?"

"Alice. I'm Sara's grandmother's grandmother, following the female line back." She walked on top of a log, holding her arms out to the side. "I forgot how much I enjoy walking in the woods." She hopped down. "I know your mother. She had magic before she died. It became stronger in the afterlife. Our family has been watching your family for a long time." When Em remained silent, she said, "I know the question you want to ask. You want to know if there's a world where your mother is still alive."

"Is there?" Em met her gaze with tears in her eyes.

"I haven't seen one." She put her arm around Em's shoulders. "Emma and Dawn believe the parallel worlds began with them, but it actually began with your mother.

Until she died, all of you were in one world. Soon after, Donna and Monna went their separate ways. You lasted longer. You created your own world in high school. The differences were small, but none of you wanted to be reminded of your mother. It was too emotional. So, you each chose a different name for your friends to call you. Your family's magic made it possible for such minor changes to create whole new worlds. What I can't work out is how Sara replaced Cassie and Candra in your world. They have no family in common, and I can't find a version of Cassie who belongs here."

"Maybe she died." Em stopped and stared at the ground. "The path is gone."

Christa/Sara stared at the path. It blinked a few times and disappeared. Em noticed immediately, but she didn't notice the other changes. The ground was dry, but now it was wet. It was several degrees cooler as well. However, the biggest change was the sound. She heard the hum of electricity. They were near a town. "Em," she said. "We're in another world."

Em looked around. "What? How?" She shivered when a gust of wind hit them.

"I don't know, but I feel a storm coming," Christa/Sara said." She pointed to the right. "That way. There's a town. Do you hear the hum of the electricity?"

Em shook her head. "But I trust you."

They walked in silence for several minutes, stopping several times to listen for the hum. As they got closer, Em pointed to her ear and nodded. After a few more minutes, they saw a glow of light over a hill. "The diner?" Em mouthed.

Christa/Sara shook her head as she saw lightning shoot from the ground to the sky. "I think we found Harvey." She walked until she could see what was creating the lightning. "We're not in another world. He brought a piece here from another place."

Em joined her at the top of the hill and looked down. "Is it from here or from another world?" She peered down at the building at the center of the lightning. It was half a building. She imagined it was what a building would look like if someone used a giant laser to cut it in half. Christa/Sara stood tall and walked down the hill. Em hurried after her. "What are you doing? Harvey's down there."

"I don't think so," Christa/Sara said. "I think he lured Mother to another place and trapped her in that building. She used her power to bring herself and as much of the building as she could to the center of the island where she's strongest. I think she's still trapped. The lightning is her fighting to free herself." She handed the radio to Em. "Call the others. We need everyone here so we can save her."

After a moment fidgeting with the radio and with a little help from Christa/Sara, Em held the button and spoke to the others. "Sara and I need everyone at the center of the island. We found Mother, and she's trapped."

When no one responded, Christa/Sara said, "Release the button so they can talk."

When she released the button, she heard Cassie and then Candra say they were headed their way. Then Maddie's voice came over the radio. "Are you where the lightning is? I can come, but we found Sara's and Regina's bodies. We were about to revive Sara."

Christa/Sara grabbed the radio from Em and spoke to Maddie. "Not yet. I need to be here and help Mother first. If you revive me, I will be pulled back. I don't know how long it will take to adjust. Maddie, come as quickly as you can. Leave Emma and Dawn to guard my body."

Emma's voice came over the radio. "Maddie is on her way. Your body still looks alive. I don't know how - it's been days and still looks perfect. Regina's body too. Sara, watch for Maddie and keep her safe. She's alone on the trail, but we're not far away. It shouldn't take long for her to reach you."

Christa/Sara hooked the radio on her belt. "I know why Harvey wants my body preserved, but why preserve Regina's body? He killed her because he didn't need Eme anymore."

"He wants it for someone else." Em stared at the building down the hill where Mother was trapped. "I think he wants to trap Mother in Regina's body."

Christa/Sara's eyes went wide. "It's the only way he can rule all the worlds."

* * *

Christa/Sara hiked to the top of the hill when everyone except Maddie had arrived to help. She should have been the first one there. "Maybe she's lost," Christa said inside her head.

Christa/Sara shook her head. "Something's wrong," she whispered. "Maddie saw the lightning. She knows exactly where we are."

Monna joined her at the top of the hill. "I can feel him. He came after me first before my world was destroyed. I can feel his anger."

They heard the scream an instant before the ground shook. "Maddie!" They both yelled.

"Everyone, go!" It was Mother's voice. "Save Maddie!"

Christa/Sara was already running in the direction of the scream. The others followed her. When they reached a clearing, Christa/Sara saw Maddie sprawled on the ground. Next to her, Eme in the body of the young woman with half blond and half blue hair, held her arms up. Christa/Sara didn't see Harvey until she looked up. He was hanging in the air several feet above their heads.

"Eme, what are you doing? We may need him to free Mother," Donna said.

"That's not Eme." Christa/Sara walked over and checked on Maddie. "She's alive." She stood and looked up at Harvey. He was rigid. She looked at the woman holding him aloft. "Are you Nikki?"

"Yes." The woman's arms shook, and Harvey dropped a couple feet. "He's strong. I need help."

In the borrowed bodies of the girl gang; Sara, Victoria, and Nathan stood with Nikki, forming a circle around Harvey. "Monna," Victoria said. "You have a connection with him. Come stand in the circle with us."

She stood out with her completely blond hair among the young women who all had blue in their hair in varying amounts. She copied them and raised her hands. Harvey rose a few feet. "What now?" she asked.

"We drop him on the building where Mother's trapped," Nathan said.

As the group moved slowly towards the building, Em, Donna, and Cassie picked up Maddie. It took all three of them to carry her safely. Em held her shoulders while Donna and Cassie held her hips and legs. As they walked, Candra guided the way. "I guess Emma and Dawn are with Sara's body," Candra said.

"I'm sure Emma wants to revive her as soon as she can," Donna said. "If I was her, I would be waiting for a call on the radio."

Cassie laughed. "Technically, you are her."

As they neared the building, Cassie almost dropped Maddie's legs. "Maybe we should stop here. It looks like the others are stopping." They found a dry and relatively flat spot and laid Maddie down. "They must be talking in each other's heads." She gestured to the others. "Do you think it will work?"

"I'm not sure about their plan," Candra said. "They drop him, and then what?"

No one answered. Cassie shrugged.

In one swift movement, the group flung their arms down then back up. Harvey flew up before falling onto the building. The glow intensified for an instant as they watched him break through the barrier. A spark exited as he vanished through the barrier and flew to Maddie.

Candra jumped as Maddie sat up. "He's trapped now," Mother and Maddie said together. "Look. He's trying to escape." Lightning rippled in and around the building.

"Will he be able to get out?" Em asked.

"I strengthened the cage with my own magic while inside," Mother said. "He won't be getting out."

"Are we going to leave him there?" Monna asked.

"Yes," Mother said. "He already died once when I destroyed his world. I'm sending him back where he belongs. If he knows what's good for him, he'll stay dead this time."

Christa/Sara watched for a short time before she called Emma and Dawn on the radio. "You can revive me now."

"We can't," Dawn said. "We heard Mother tell us Harvey is trapped. So, we tried. It's not working. We need someone or something else. I'm sorry, Sara."

Without a word, Christa/Sara grabbed Em's hand and ran to Emma and Dawn. On the way, she talked into the radio. "I'm on my way with Em. I have an idea."

* * *

Dawn and Emma stood next to Sara's body. "Where is Regina's body?" Christa/Sara asked. Dawn pointed off to the side. "Help me move her."

"Nikki said Regina can't come back. She's moved on," Emma said. "Don't tell me you plan to bring back Eme."

Christa/Sara shook her head. "No, but I need a failsafe. If I can't use my body, I will take hers."

"And if she takes it first?" Dawn asked.

"I will fight for it." Christa/Sara grabbed Regina's shoulders. "Someone get her feet." Em grabbed the feet when the others didn't move.

"I understand you're frightened," Em said. "But I trust Sara, and we need to do this quickly. Harvey is trapped. If something happens to him, we won't have long. I don't want to lose her again. Please."

"Wait!" Mother's voice boomed all around them. "You will have all the time you need, but I need Regina's body for someone else. Nathan and Victoria will help my husband slow time on the island. I need Emma to come with me."

"Why do you need me?" Emma asked.

"You most resemble the one I need to save. We must go now." As Emma disappeared, Mother said, "Sara, I promise we will return momentarily."

Chapter 22

Prayers Answered

Emma saw darkness for a moment before she appeared in a hospital room. When she felt Mother join her, the room brightened. A dark-haired young woman looked up as she sat at the bedside of another version of herself. In her head, Mother spoke to her. "I need to speak to her. Stand back in the shadows. It should only be a short time for you. I need to know if she wants to be saved. Sometimes people don't want to fight for it. Regina was like that." Emma nodded and stood in the corner of the room.

Mother spoke face to face with her daughter inside her head. The others only heard her voice, but now she appeared as a vision. "Madena, my daughter, you're dying."

"I know. I can feel it. Are you here to take me away?" she asked.

"I don't want to." Mother folded herself around Madena. "It's your choice. "If you can fight and hold on for a little longer, I can save you." She sent her love out to Madena. "But I won't waste my energy if you're going to give up. I know you're weak and tired, but I can give you a new body."

"What happens if I can't hold on?"

"Then you will come with me. You will become an angel, and you can return to watch over your children. If you fight for your life, I can give you back twenty years of your life. If I do, you must promise to take care of yourself."

"I want to live." Madena said.

"That's the daughter I know. Promise me you won't neglect your health again."

"I promise. For you, I will take care of myself."

"Not for me," Mother said. "For your children."

"For my children. I want to live a long life for them. I love them more than anything."

"Good. Now I need you to hold on while I speak with my granddaughter."

"Tell her I love her more than anything."

Emma cried as she listened to Mother's conversation in her head. She didn't know if it was intentional that she left the connection intact.

The room lit up with warm light as Mother spoke. "I heard your prayers, Laurel. I'm here to save your mother."

She had not seen Emma. Looking up at the ceiling, she asked. "Why?"

Mother's light wrapped around Laurel. "She is my daughter. You are my granddaughter, and I won't let you lose her."

Laurel wiped tears from her eyes. "They tell me she's going to be okay, but I don't believe them."

"Look behind you."

When she turned and saw Emma, she gasped. "How? I don't understand."

"She is your mother from a different world. She will stay here with you while I take your mother with me. When I return, your mother will have a new body. You must keep this a secret. Don't let anyone examine her too closely. I know the nurses already checked her. They shouldn't return before I do."

"I think I understand. Does my mother know you're here?"

"Yes, and she wants you to know how much she loves you, but you must let her go so she can come back to you," Mother said.

Laurel nodded. "Thank you."

In less than a second, Emma found herself in the bed wearing a hospital gown and hooked to all the machines. "Hurry."

* * *

Christa/Sara finished moving Regina's body to lie a couple feet away from her own. Nathan and Victoria healed small wounds on the body and changed the hair color to blond. Someone removed the colored contacts. When it was all done, the body looked amazingly like Emma. It all took less than a minute. Before she finished, Mother had returned with an extremely ill woman.

"This is my first daughter from the world where I died. She doesn't have long. When you revive the bodies, I will guide her soul into Regina's body. Then I must take her back to my granddaughter. Whatever you have planned, do it now."

Em sat on the ground between the two bodies. "I hope this works because this is weird, even for me."

Christa/Sara sat in front of her. "Remember the electricity when I kissed you earlier. I think we use that to revive the bodies. Now lie back." She pushed Em down and lay on top of her. "I think it would help if we actually touched them."

Dawn pushed the bodies close enough to touch on each side.

"I'm supposed to ignore them?" Em asked.

"Focus on me," Christa/Sara said. "Try to forget I'm in another body. Try to ignore everyone around us." She bent her head and kissed her. When Em didn't respond, she sent a trickle of her new magic through her fingers as she caressed her side. Em wrapped her arms around Christa/Sara and held her tight as they both poured their hearts into the kiss.

The air crackled all around, and both of them glowed. Sara reached out with both hands and touched the hearts on her and Regina's bodies. Electricity flowed through her and sent a jolt into the bodies. She felt both hearts beating. Then she was floating.

When Sara opened her eyes, she was staring up at the sky. As she turned her head, she saw Em and Christa. "You can stop kissing my wife now." She propped herself up on her elbows and looked over at Regina's body. She was struggling to sit up, but Dawn was helping. It occurred to her that Mother didn't give them the name of this version of her daughter. They probably all knew the name, but no one wanted to be the first to speak it.

"How are you feeling?" Dawn asked her, as she helped her stand.

Madena stared at the lifeless body she once inhabited. "Glad to be alive. I don't understand any of this. Is she really my mother?"

Dawn nodded. "Our mother. After she died, she continued to watch over you and all of us in multiple universes. It's complicated. If you need her, just pray. She's not God, but she hears us."

* * *

Emma wasn't in the hospital room long before a nurse came running. She guessed that the nurse must have seen the interruption on the monitors when she switched places with the other version of herself. She tried to calm herself, but her heart was racing. That brought more people into check on her.

Before anyone could ask questions or check on her, she was standing, and the other woman was in the bed. Mother was in her head again. "I'm only here to help," she said as she began to glow.

Mother shushed her and spoke in her head. "Face them and let me speak."

When she turned, she glowed brighter, and the nurse at the front gasped. "An angel."

As Mother spoke through her, Emma listened to murmurs from the medical team. "Madena is alive and well," Mother said. "You may run tests, but you will find no infection. She is as healthy as someone twenty years younger."

A nurse raised her hand. "Are you actually an Angel?"

Mother spoke directly to her. "I suppose that's what I have been since I died." She pointed to the bed behind her. "She is my daughter, and I heard her prayers as she was dying. I came and saved her. I had hoped to do it secretly, but now you know."

A man near the door cleared his throat. "No one will believe this."

Emma saw most of them with phones out pointed at them. Behind her, she heard the bed creak behind her as people gasped.

Mother turned and helped Madena to her feet. "My daughter, I love you so much. If you need me again, I'm only a thought away." She turned to Laurel. "My granddaughter, you have grown into a lovely young woman. I'm proud of how you stayed by your mother's side. I believe you helped her hold onto life until I could save her." She kissed each of their cheeks. "Don't push yourself so hard. People will love you even if you're not perfect. Listen to your heart. It will lead you in the right direction."

As Mother turned back, Emma saw that the door was open. Dozens of people crowded around with their phones. Mother spoke to them and the world watching the live streams. "I love you all. Thank you for loving and supporting my daughter and her family. I heard all the prayers. I couldn't have saved her without you. Please, treat her well. There is no one else like her in this world."

As people shouted questions, the room disappeared, and Emma appeared in front of Dawn in the clearing. Dawn pulled her into a hug as she felt arms wrap around her from behind. "I'm glad you're back," Maddie said.

"How long was I gone?" Emma asked. "It shouldn't have been that long."

"I think my husband had trouble keeping time steady here," Mother said to everyone.

"It's been a week," Dawn said. "Nathan realized there was a problem and took us to Em's house. He brought us back when he felt Mother returning."

"Why not take me to you?" Emma asked.

"We need to take care of Harvey and Eme here," Sara said.

"I have a plan for Eme," Mother said. "Where is she?"

"Victoria, Nathan, and Nikki have her in that place between worlds," Sara said. "We thought she'd be safe there until you returned."

Chapter 23

The Wedding Concert

"Are you going to make me stay dead?" Eme asked. "Sara went back. Why can't I?"

Mother let the question hang in the air as she considered her answer. "Sara had a body to return to that was hers. That body wasn't yours. In fact, you never had a body of your own. You were a separate soul in Emma's body. I don't think it's fair to her to put you back there."

"But you put someone else into Regina's body. I don't understand. Do you hate me?"

Even in the darkness of the place between worlds, she could see Eme. Her soul was bright. "I have a plan for you. I need you to watch over my daughter and her children."

"Which one?" Eme asked.

"You know which one," Mother said.

"The one in Regina's body." Eme stayed silent for a long time before saying, "Okay. What about Harvey?"

"Let me worry about him."

* * *

Sara looked out over the seating area. The only place for it was over the water, but the stage crew and set builders assured her it was safe. She guessed it was the only logical place for the audience since they built the stage on the bridge.

"I heard that Madena is coming," Dawn said as she looked around the stage. "Why does that make me nervous?"

"Don't overthink it. I know you were scared to talk with Emma before you got to know her. Just think of Madena as a long lost sister." Sara turned and looked over the stage. "Are you going to sing?"

Dawn nodded. "Are you?"

Sara smiled. "I have to or else the magic won't work. Everyone can choose which songs to perform, but I need to be onstage for all of them and sing along."

"Are you scared?" Em asked from behind her.

Sara flinched. "Terrified, but this is how we will defeat Harvey. My magic will protect everyone who hears the music. Harvey won't have a way to influence them. The magic will block him. That's why we need to reach as many worlds as we can."

Em hugged her from behind. "If it makes you feel better, we all get stage fright too. Some of us more than others. It's part of performing. I'll be with you. Don't worry."

"So, who is officiating the weddings?" Dawn asked. "I know it can't be Maddie this time."

"Mother was going to ask Madena to do it, but Emma will do it if she refuses." Sara turned around and kissed Em. "I know we're married now, but maybe we should do it again since I died and came back. I think it would help the magic."

"Someone else died and came back?"

Sara and Em turned to see who had spoken. The woman looked similar to Maddie, but she carried herself with more confidence. "Madena?" Sara asked. She glanced at Em and whispered, "We really need a visual way of telling everyone apart, especially on stage." Sara looked back at the newcomer. She looked the same age as Maddie, but Sara knew that was because of her new body. Her soul was decades older. Even without makeup and wearing jeans and a t-shirt, she was beautiful. Behind her was a team of people with racks of clothes, and, she assumed, makeup and jewelry.

"Yes. I'm Madena. Mother said I didn't need to participate, but it's the least I can do after she saved my life." She pointed to the clothes. "I brought what I could on short notice. Clothes, shoes, makeup, jewelry, whatever you need. My stylists came with me. We can each have our own style."

"I don't suppose you have anything that could be used as wedding dresses?" Sara walked to the racks at the end of the bridge. "I don't know what happened to the one Em had made for me. We do still have the two that Monna and Candra wore, but we need five total."

"Who is going to wear the rainbow dress?" Dawn asked.

"Cassie said I could wear it if we joined the ceremony," Sara said. "But we know it will fit her perfectly since Candra wore it."

"You will look beautiful whatever you wear." Em looked through a section of silver dresses and pulled one out. "I like this one. If I can wear Monna's pinstripe dress, this would go beautifully with it."

Madena handed Sara silver boots. "Mother suggested this dress with these boots."

Sara took the boots as she stared at the dress. It was a similar style to Cassie's dress, but the colors were different. Cassie's was mostly pink with a bright rainbow underskirt and silver accents. This had pale rainbow swirls on silver metallic fabric but still had the bright rainbow underskirt and silver ruffled trim.

Madena pulled out another dress like it but made with purple silk. "This is for Maddie."

"Where did these come from?" Sara asked. "There couldn't have been time to have them made."

"I don't fully understand," Madena said. "But Mother put a time bubble around the place you work. Your coworkers made these. Candra's coworkers, saved from her world, helped." She pulled out two more items. "This is your dress, Em."

Em took the white dress with gold and black pinstripes. It also had the corset with gold buckles. "Thank you." She gestured to the other hanger. "Is that for John?"

"Yes." Madena nodded and showed them the tuxedo. It was white and gold with purple pinstripes to match Maddie's dress. She hung the tuxedo on the rack and walked over to Dawn. "I haven't forgotten you or Emma. I want you to pick anything you want." She turned back to Sara. "Mother told me you're the one in charge of the show. When do we rehearse?"

Sara shook her head. "No rehearsal because of the magic, except the first song. We need to rehearse choreography for the first song without any singing. The dancing is magic when put together with the vocals. It needs to be as precise as possible. When we start, everyone needs to sing it. If the audience sings, that will help. Absolutely no improvising on the first song. The wedding will follow the first song." She waited for a response, but continued when she didn't get one. "Look. I know you're used to being in charge, and everyone here is used to deferring to Emma. But I know the magic. If you would feel better planning out the songs after the wedding, I would be happy to let you do that. Just know that I need to sing at least part of every song. Please run the song list by me before we start."

"Are you always this bossy?" Madena asked.

"Only since Harvey killed her," Em said.

"Did Mother bring you back?" Madena asked.

"No," Sara said. "I brought myself back."

* * *

"We're live on all social media platforms and several television networks. Mother says we're live in all the worlds she connected," John said.

Sara nodded. "Start the music."

The music started with a quiet melody played on the keyboard as the lights lit up the stage. The crowd went wild when they saw ten of them onstage all dressed in white shirts and pants. When the drums and guitars started, they danced and sang in unison. Energy flowed around them in rainbows. Each time they moved the rainbows followed. Soon, they broke off into individual dances as they sang in harmony. The magic was guiding them. When people in the crowd joined in singing, the rainbows flowed out to hover above them. Soon, the night was bright as the air crackled with the magic. As the song ended, they danced together in the center of the stage. As one, they thrust their hands towards the sky. All the rainbows shot upwards as lightning rippled through the sky.

As the crowd cheered, and the lightning provided light, they hurried to change into the clothes for the remainder of the show. When they returned to the stage dressed for the wedding, the audience was silent. The last rumbles of thunder echoed all around them.

"You just witnessed magic," Madena said. "Now we invite you to witness a wedding. Three couples stand before you: Donna and Cassie, Em and Sara, John and Maddie. I am Madena, and I am proud to have the honor of joining their hearts together in marriage tonight."

Monna, Emma, and Dawn joined them. Each stood by one of the couples and held gold and silver ribbons. "Each of you take your partner's hand in yours." As one they reached with their left hands and grasped their partners' hands. Monna, Emma, and Dawn threaded the ends of the ribbons between their hands before wrapping them around their arms. They wrapped silver on Donna, Em, and John; and they wrapped gold on Cassie, Sara, and Maddie.

Carrying a rainbow pillow, Candra joined them. One at a time, she handed rings from the pillow to Madena who placed the rings on the fingers of each of the six getting married. After each ring was placed, the ribbon on their partner's arm glowed. When she finished, she stepped back. "The rings will remain as they are, but the gold and silver will become a part of them, forever linking their hearts and souls." The ribbons glowed brighter before vanishing, leaving gold and silver trails around their arms.

"You may wonder why they haven't exchanged vows," Madena said. "But they have. Words aren't necessary. They have made vows with their hearts. I recognize that and acknowledge that these three couples are now married. Let them seal their vows with a kiss."

The three couples leaned in and kissed. The air crackled around them. Lightning shot to the sky, and thunder boomed. The audience clapped and cheered.

When the couples parted, Madena stepped forward. "Now. We celebrate."

* * *

Sara's heart pounded as music replaced the booming thunder. "Before we celebrate, you need to know who we are. Every fan knows the name Madena." She looked over her shoulder at Madena. "In other worlds, she uses other names: Dawn, Emma, Maddie, Em, Monna, and Donna." Each of them stepped forward as Sara said their name. "As fans in her world know, Madena was extremely ill. She was attacked by an evil man, Harvey. We don't know how he reached her, but his magic spread through her quickly. It seemed as if she had an infection, but his magic took her life. Her mother …"

"Our mother too," Em said.

Sara nodded. "Mother went to her as she died and saved her." She waited for the crowd to react with gasps and cries. "Her world believes Mother is an angel, but she is much more. She is here with us all today."

As the others began singing quietly, Em took Sara's hand. "As many saw in my world, Harvey also took Sara from me. He killed her as my world watched. Her family waited for her between worlds when she died and helped her come back to me. She returned with magic. Tonight, we will use her magic and our music to fight the hate that Harvey spreads. He wants to rule all the worlds with hate, and we can't let that happen."

"Wherever you are tonight, sing along and spread the love." Sara raised her hand and Em's. "Fight the hate." The music became louder as Em led her in dancing, leaving her to focus on the magic. She knew the music and sang without thinking about it.

The initial magic had done its job. Even without seeing Harvey. She knew he was unconscious. Until the lightning had reached him, she had felt his presence. Even from his prison, he had reached her. It had taken all her strength to keep him out of her mind. Now, she sent that strength to everyone through the music. Em, along with the others on stage, sent love. Everyone hearing the music felt the love. Sara used that connection to give them strength to resist the hate Harvey spread.

Sara wasn't an experienced performer, but the audience didn't seem to notice. With each song, she sang with a different person or group of them. The magic built with every note. She could feel the emotions as they rode the wave of magic out into the crowd and through the cameras to the people watching in all the worlds.

Like the concert the day she died, they needed to continue for several hours to allow as many people as possible to watch and experience the magic live. After they performed the final song at sunrise, Sara collapsed on the stage from exhaustion. The others had opportunities to rest, but she had kept the magic flowing for every song.

Security was overwhelmed as the audience poured onto the stage and surrounded Sara. One young woman grabbed Em and had her hold Sara's hand before holding Sara's other hand. Soon, they formed a chain, holding hands until Madena grabbed Em's other hand. "We need to give her strength." The voice from the young woman was more mature than Em expected, and she suspected she was hearing Victoria or Nikki.

The stage and surrounding area glowed bright as day as they all joined together singing one more song. The light grew until it covered the island. In the distance, a dark cloud rose into the sky and moved towards them. Em could see a person thrashing around in the middle of it. It stopped directly above Sara. "Harvey."

When the music stopped, the young woman said, "He is weak, and his power is diminished. But he is too dangerous to leave here. We will take him. Nathan has prepared a prison for him between worlds where he can't harm anyone." A ball of light left her and pushed the dark cloud away.

A few at a time, people released their hands, breaking the chain. Em helped Sara to her feet and embraced her. "We did it."

Chapter 24

Who Wants to Rule the Worlds?

For months after the concert, videos were shared daily in all the worlds. People talked about it on the street as much as they did online.

Dawn sat next to Emma in the diner and waited for the others to arrive for their weekly brunch. The television on the wall showed happy news stories. Crime was down. They no longer saw daily reports of shootings, not even weekly incidents since Harvey was taken away. One news story that Dawn saw almost daily should have been a happy story, but she didn't see it that way.

Once everyone arrived, Dawn muted the television. "Before we eat, Emma and I have an issue to discuss." She looked around at Madena, Monna, Candra, Donna, Cassie, Em, Sara, and John. "Where's Maddie?"

"She'll be here soon," he said. "She's sick this morning."

"Anything serious?" Emma asked.

Maddie walked in with her hand on her stomach. "Nothing that won't be better in a few months. Don't worry about me. I'm okay." She sat next to John. "What are we discussing?"

Emma took a sip of coffee. "We need to address the issue of the desire for a universal leader. I know it wasn't our intention when we held the multidimensional concert months ago. Harvey wanted to rule over all the worlds. Even before the concert, the public called for some of us to run for political office. We all resisted the idea."

"But now," Dawn said. "Leaders of nations in multiple worlds have started asking for one of us to step into a universal leadership role."

"They want one of us to be Queen of all the worlds?" Maddie asked.

"I heard my president suggest that I could be an Empress," Donna said.

"I fear unrest if we don't make a statement in response to this," Em said.

"What about the music?" Cassie asked. "Wouldn't it leave one world without your music?"

The diner fell into an uncomfortable silence. After a long moment, Sara was the first to speak. "None of us have experience with politics. Maybe that's good. People don't need politics. They need leadership. I think they want one of us, but they didn't specify which one. They didn't say it couldn't be Cassie, Candra, or me, and they didn't suggest anyone not in this room."

"We can't just pick one of us and make a declaration of Empress or Queen." Monna looked around at everyone. "Can we? That would be what Harvey wanted to do."

Madena stood. "There should be an election. To be fair, there needs to be a choice that's not one of us, and we need more than one of us. I suggest Emma and Sara if we do this at all."

"I don't want that responsibility," Sara said. "I'm sure Emma feels the same."

Emma nodded. "I wouldn't mind being a figurehead, but ruling over everything isn't me. I don't think any of us would like that job."

Candra cleared her throat. "So, we respond with the suggestion of figureheads. It seems to me that people want all of us, not one or two." She tapped her fingers on the table. "I know Harvey should be locked away for good, but just in case he ever escapes, we can do a concert once or twice a year to renew the magic. We could make it into a ceremony."

Sara glanced at Em. "I think it's a good idea." She bent her head and played with her coffee cup. "There's something else. I probably should have talked to Em first, but here's another problem. If anything happens to me again, the magic protection will fade. It's passed down through the women in my family. Nathan strengthened it and gave me more magic, but if I die, there's no one else with the magic."

"Isn't there a version of you in another world?" Cassie asked. "We can find her."

"I don't know why, but I'm the only one of me. Mother has looked in thousands of worlds." Sara took Em's hand. "I have a plan. It's the other reason I don't want to be a leader." She looked around at everyone. "I need to have a baby. I need a daughter. Nathan said my family mostly has girls. It's part of the magic. But I need a man to be the father."

Everyone turned and looked at John and Maddie. "Oh no," Maddie said as she scooted closer to John. "You are not having sex with my husband."

John patted Maddie's hand. "I'm sure there's another way."

* * *

Em held Sara's hand as she stared up at the ceiling. "Nervous?"

Sara shook her head. "No, but I think John is." She turned her head and watched as Maddie bent over John and whispered something in his ear. He smiled and nodded.

Emma stepped between the beds and spoke in Mother's voice. "Are you ready?"

"Yes," Sara and John said.

With a nod, Emma reached to each side and took their hands in hers. Em released Sara's other hand and stepped back as John, Sara, and Emma glowed. As Emma brought Sara's and John's hands together between both of hers, the light surrounding them swirled.

In moments, it was over, and John tried to sit up. Emma pushed him down. "Stay still and rest," she said in Mother's voice. "You're not accustomed to the magic. It will take several minutes to recover." She placed a hand on Sara's shoulder. "It will take longer for you. Rest for an hour or two." She looked Em in the eye until she nodded her understanding.

"Where are the others?" Maddie asked.

"They are preparing to broadcast our intentions to the worlds," Mother said. "They may need us."

* * *

Emma and Madena watched the computer monitors along the wall of the diner. There was one for each world they would be speaking to. "I still don't understand why they're showing different dates." Madena pointed to one screen "This one shows a date almost twenty years earlier than the day I died."

"That's Maddie's world," Emma said. "Mother froze time there when Maddie was caught in the glitch and traveling between worlds. That world is ten years earlier than mine." She pointed to one of the screens. "Try not to think about it too much. It'll give you a headache. I'm thankful that the magic of the island has synced time in all the worlds. While it's a different year in each, they're all moving forward at the same speed now."

"Who set this up?" Madena asked.

"Dawn set up the computers. Sara and Mother connected them to the different worlds." Emma touched a bright colored sticker under one of the monitors. "It was Dawn's idea to assign a color to each world." She touched each sticker as she looked at the screens. "Maddie and John are green. Donna and Cassie are red. Em and Sara are pink. You are gold. Monna and Candra's world was destroyed. They have been living here on the island with Dawn and me. Our island is the blue computer." She tapped her finger on a screen with an orange sticker. "I don't know what world this is."

"That's Regina's world."

Madena turned to see Dawn behind them. "Regina?"

Dawn waved her hand up and down. "You're in her body. She chose to move on when Harvey killed her. Mother used her body to save you." She typed on a keyboard and clicked the mouse a few times. The screen changed to show a young girl walking in a park.

Madena touched the screen. "That looks like Laurel when she was younger."

"Mother has visited her many times. She is well taken care of."

"I want to expand my tour. If they know about us, I should perform there."

"Dawn, do they know Regina died?" Emma asked. "Do they know about us?"

"Yes. Mother broadcast the concert to their world with all the others. She wanted to keep them safe."

"Madena, you can plan that after the big concert." Emma turned at the sound of the door opening. "Right now, we need to talk to all the world leaders."

Maddie and John walked in and sat at the counter. "Did we find translators for everyone?" Maddie asked.

Dawn joined her at the counter. "Most of the leaders have their own translators, and Nathan found a magical way to translate for the smaller nations. He tried to explain, but I didn't understand. I understand the computers, but magic is Sara's thing."

"What's my thing?" Sara walked in leaning on Em. Her face was paler than usual.

"Magic," Dawn said. "Are you okay? You don't look so good."

Sara waved away the question as Em answered for her. "She's a little queasy from the magic." She leaned close to

Sara's ear and whispered, "I told you to rest a while longer. The worlds can wait."

"I'm okay." Sara sat in the nearest chair. "I just need a moment. If they can't handle some of us sitting down, that's their problem."

"We should all sit." Madena started arranging chairs in front of the counter. Emma joined her. The barstools were tall enough that anyone sitting on them could be seen behind those sitting in the chairs. Dawn and Em moved the cameras to face the counter. The computer monitors were mounted on a rack that was moved to the appropriate wall. "That's better," Madena said. "If they want us, they can do things our way."

"Wait," Maddie said. "We're not thinking of accepting the offer to rule everything. Are we? I thought we decided not to do that."

"No, but if we're going to be public figures of inspiration for all of them, I don't want them to dictate how we do it. I won't be a pawn." Madena smiled. "I've never allowed myself to be a pawn for anyone."

"Oh. This is a different setup." Cassie said as she walked into the diner with Donna, Monna, and Candra.

"We will broadcast only," Dawn said as she took her seat between Emma and Maddie. "It's easier than trying to manage two-way communication with so many worlds."

John stood behind the camera. "We will record and broadcast every six hours for twenty-four hours to be sure everyone sees it." He smiled at Maddie and counted down. "Five, four, three, two, one." He gave a thumbs up.

Madena, sitting in the center front chair, spoke. "It has come to our attention that people everywhere have been asking us to become leaders for all of you. We understand the need to be united in peace, to spread love, and to stand against hate. We want to be symbols for that, but we don't wish to rule over anyone." She raised a photo. "These are my children." She held up another photo. "This is my daughter in a different world. We have families."

Donna, Em, and Emma held up photos of their adult children. Monna and Maddie held up photos of their younger children.

"Some of our children are adults," Madena said. "Some are still adolescents or teenagers, but they all need us. We can't spare the time to care for all of you as well. We don't think any of the worlds are prepared to have one common ruler or even a group of us leading everyone."

Sara spoke from behind Madena. "We want to be an inspiration to everyone, symbols for peace. In one week, it will be six months since our last combined concert. We will perform another to keep the love alive in all our worlds. If we fill everyone with love, there's no room for hate."

"It is our plan to do this every six months," Madena said. "We hope this is an acceptable compromise. All the worlds treat us like royalty. We accept that, but we do not want to be political or spiritual leaders. It's too much."

With a gesture of his hand, John told them the camera was off. "We're done," he said. He walked over to check on Maddie and Sara. "Do you think it was safe to mention the children?"

Sara nodded. "All of them except Madena's live here on the island where Mother can better protect them."

Madena stood. "Don't worry, John. I have a lot of experience keeping my children safe. If necessary, I will move them here. No one should know how to find Regina's daughter." She held up a photo. "This isn't a photo of her daughter. It's my daughter, Laurel, when she was younger. I wouldn't put Regina's daughter at risk, even if we're sure Harvey is still in his prison."

* * *

Em threw her hands in the air. "They want a coronation! From the message I saw, they believe it will bring peace if there's a coronation. Why? It won't change a thing."

Emma sat sipping her coffee silently for a moment. "I suppose it's like when two countries seal a peace treaty with a marriage. There's always a coronation as well as a wedding."

Em fell into a chair at the counter. "We had a wedding six months ago."

Dawn sat a cup of coffee on the counter for Em before sitting with Emma at the table. "I think a coronation would make it feel like all of us were married to one another, like a group marriage. One husband, John, and ten wives. I know it's weird, but it could work."

"As long as we're not expected to consummate all the different pairings." Em shuddered.

Emma shook her head. "I'm sure that's not the intention. If it is, I'm sure Mother will find a magical way to satisfy the requirement. Otherwise, we negotiate. We already went down this road once with Eme.

"Any idea who they want to crown us?" Dawn asked.

"They didn't say, but the date is special." Emma smiled. "They want to do it this Saturday."

Chapter 25

Long Live the Queens

Sara never saw so many cameras. She couldn't believe Emma and Madena allowed so many reporters from all the worlds. With help from Mother, she connected each camera to the appropriate world. By the time she finished, she was shaking. With a hand around her waist, Em helped her to a chair away from the crowd and sat next to her.

"You need to stop occasionally and rest before you collapse." Em brushed a lock of hair out of Sara's eyes. "We've planned breaks in the concert later. We can't allow you to push yourself to extremes like last time." She put her hand on Sara's stomach. "How are you feeling?"

Sara put her hand over Em's. "I'm good." She smiled. "I saw Maddie earlier. She's much better."

"I think Mother worked some magic."

"Speaking of magic," Sara said. "Do we have an answer from Madena? She's more private than the rest of you. I need to know if she has a partner. Will the coronation have eleven or twelve of us? John doesn't sing. If Madena has a partner who sings, there will be eleven performing. It will affect the magic."

Em shook her head. "There was someone with her when I saw her this morning, but I don't know who they are." She looked at her phone when it buzzed. "They're ready for us."

With a nod, Sara stood. As they made their way to the stage, security followed them. People reached out and touched them. They touched hands when they could, and people cried. "It's different now." Sara kept her voice quiet. "They're more than fans."

Em leaned close and whispered, "Reverence. Awe. Respect."

"I'm not sure I'm ready for that." Sara stopped, causing security to bump into her. She stared at a woman who looked exactly like her. "Who is she?"

From behind her, she heard John answer. "She came with Madena. Her name is Sophie. She looks a lot like you. I thought you didn't have a duplicate."

"That's what we were told." Em held Sara's hand as they walked towards Sophie.

Before they could introduce themselves, Madena stepped up to them. "Sara, Em, I want you to meet Sophie."

Sara stared at Sophie. "Mother said she couldn't find another version of me. What's going on?"

Madena smiled. "Mother checked many worlds but forgot about mine. I found Sophie through social media, or rather, she found me. She liked and commented on so many posts that I had to find her."

Sophie blushed. "I was writing a book and doing research for my characters. When she showed up at my door, I realized it was all real."

Em nudged Sara with her elbow. "Sounds like what happened with us."

Sophie looked at Madena and smiled. "I know. I wrote all about Sara writing her book and you reading it and falling in love with her before Harvey showed up and disrupted your lives. I wrote all about them too." She pointed at the stage.

"Do you sing?" Sara blurted out. "Oh, and are you part of the coronation? It would make the magic easier. Assuming you have magic like I do."

Sophie looked down at her feet as she thought for a moment. "Yes, I sing. I don't know about the coronation. I don't know if I have magic."

Madena put her arm around Sophie. "Don't let her be modest. She has vocal training. She knows how to sing and knows almost all my songs which means she knows yours too." She looked at Sophie. "I would love for you to be part of the coronation."

Sophie smiled at Madena. "I'm not that good. I took lessons years ago when I was in my school choir. I haven't performed in over thirty years."

"You'll be fine. If I can perform with Em, you can do it. You won't be alone." Sara waved at Emma who came over right away. "We need to move Madena to the end opposite me and put Sophie at the very end. The magic will have better harmony that way." She turned back to Sophie. "You don't have to perform everything with us, but it would help if you sang the first song with us. You will need a lesson on the choreography."

Sophie's eyes grew wide. "I don't dance."

"Don't worry. It's not really dancing. It's magic. Mother and Victoria will help you. Okay?" Sara waited for Sophie to nod. "Good. Go with Cassie, Candra, and Dawn. They're getting a choreography refresher. Remember. Don't sing until the live performance."

As Sophie walked away with Emma, Sara turned to Madena. "Are you married, or do we need a ceremony for that too?"

Smiling, Madena held up her left hand. Gold and silver lines wrapped around her arm from her knuckles to her elbow. "During the concert six months ago, Sophie was sick too. I didn't know until I returned home. Eme was sent to watch over my family and me. She kept Sophie alive until Harvey was imprisoned. She performed a handfast for us soon after that."

Sara nodded. "That will strengthen the magic."

Em put her hand around Sara's waist. "We should join the others on stage."

* * *

Soft, instrumental music played as Sara knelt facing the gathered crowd. One at a time the others knelt, ending with Sophie at the far side of the stage. A hush fell over the crowd when a warm glow descended on the stage.

"Thank you for sharing this day with us." Mother's voice spread over the crowd as the light traveled over them. "This is a special day, not only because of the coronation, but today we celebrate my daughters' birthday." A crown rose from the floor and hovered in front of Sara. "As the people of my beloved worlds have requested, my family will be the

Queens and Prince of this multiverse." The crown rose and settled on Sara's head.

Sara picked up the crown in front of her and stood. With shaking hands, she placed the crown on Em's head. In turn, Em picked up a crown and stood. Em placed the crown on Donna's head who stood and crowned Cassie. Almost dropping the crown as she stood, Cassie crowned Emma who then crowned John.

When John placed the crown on Maddie's head, light shot from both of them and joined in the air above them. When Maddie crowned Dawn, light connected Emma and Dawn. Candra's crown connected her to Cassie, and Monna's crown connected her to Donna. By the time Monna crowned Madena, the stage was bright with an almost complete rainbow above their heads.

With slow, steady movements, Madena picked up the final crown in both hands. She kissed the crown before rising to her feet. With a smile, she turned to face Sophie and kissed her cheek before placing the crown on her head. As the completed rainbow stretched from Sophie to Sara, Madena returned to her spot on the stage. Sophie shook as she stood. She reached over and took Madena's hand. Down the line, they joined hands as the crowd applauded.

Mother's voice sounded above the noise of the crowd. "I present Queen Emma, Queen Dawn, Queen Maddie, Prince John, Queen Cassie, Queen Donna, Queen Candra, Queen Monna, Queen Em, Queen Sara, Queen Sophie, and Queen Madena." The crown erupted in cheers and applause as lightning lit the sky. Thunder echoed all around. The warm glow from Mother faded, but the rainbow stayed.

The music volume increased as Sara sang the first notes to the magical song. One by one the others joined in. When the dancing began, John bowed and left the stage. As the song continued, rainbows moved and danced all around them. As they sang the final notes, they removed their crowns and held them high in the air. Rainbows shot into the sky and mixed with the lightning in one last almost-deafening clap of thunder.

Then it was pitch black and silent for a moment until spotlights lit the stage. Applause from the crowd shook the stage as the concert continued. They performed until just before midnight when John made his way onto the stage. Candra, Cassie, Sara, and Sophie joined him in singing Happy Birthday. When the crowd joined the singing, Mother's glow lit everyone as she sang too.

"Thank you, everyone, for coming together on this special day to celebrate peace and love. My daughters have a special place in my heart, but I love you all. We must continue to love one another. There will always be hate and negativity, but love is stronger. We are here to spread love whenever, wherever we can." Mother's glow slowly faded.

Emma watched as the crowd silently dispersed. "I've never had a show end this way."

Maddie stepped close to her. "Is this a good thing?" John shrugged in answer before putting his arm around her.

Em nodded. "I hope so."

"They seem content," Cassie said.

"They may be content," Sara said, "but I'm starving."

"I say we all go back to the Diner for a late dinner," Dawn said.

Monna walked past them. "I heard Eddie made a birthday cake."

"So, this seems anticlimactic." Donna took Cassie's hand as they walked offstage.

Candra shrugged. "Better than being hunted by people in helicopters."

"Will it always be like this?" Sophie asked.

Madena laughed. "I don't know. We created something new with our music and magic. It's a new beginning."

ABOUT THE AUTHOR

Shel Schneider is a writer living in Ohio with her cat. Ever since she learned to read, she loved telling herself stories. When she was twelve years old, she began writing stories with her friends. When she turned fifty years old, she was inspired to write the first novel that she felt needed to be published.

Milton Keynes UK
Ingram Content Group UK Ltd.
UKHW010643041223
433752UK00005B/327